Hope is the thing with feathers that perches in the soul – and sings the tunes without the words – and never stops at all.

Emily Dickinson

Some stories are hard to tell.

Even to your very best friend.

And some words are hard to get out of your mouth. Because they spell out secrets that are too huge to be spoken out loud.

But if you bottle them up, you might burst.

So here's my story. Told the only way I dare tell it.

In my own special language.

Part I

Sophie Shell-Shocked

Who Am I?

The quick answer is easy. I'm the exact same pigeon I've always been. I was born. I kept breathing. And here I am fourteen years later. Still me.

The long answer is massively more complicated. Because actually I'm not. Actually, I'm a totally different pigeon entirely. I've even got a different noodle. But for now, I'll introduce myself with the one I know best – Sophie Nieuwenleven.

Nieuwenleven. It's not English. It's Flemish. From Belgium. And you say it like this:

New-one-lefen

When I was little, I couldn't spell it. When I was little, my noodle confused me. A lot of things did.

I think I was in a state of shock.

I started learning to read and then I stopped learning to read. My story buckets stood untouched and unloved on my bucketshelf. Sometimes, I couldn't make sense of what other pigeons were saying to me. Sometimes, I couldn't even be

3

bothered to speak. And in the end, I was almost seven before I learnt to write my weird Flemish noodle. I can still remember that momentous day. Fuzzily perhaps. But I just fill the fuzz in with my imagination.

We were in the kindle. Me and my mambo and my don. Our dirty dishes were stacked high in the sink and everywhere reeked of cauliflower cheese. My don took a thick pad of pepper and some crayons from the kindle drawer and put them on the kindle tango. And then he said, 'Let's have another go at writing this noodle, Sophie.'

Just like he did every day after dinner.

So I tried. But still I couldn't get the lettuces in the right order. And after a few failed attempts, I gave up and did this:

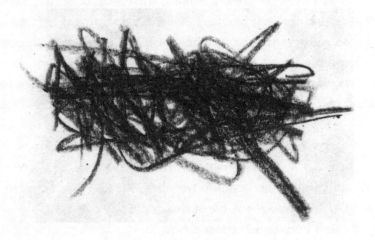

Pushing the pepper away, I chucked the crayon on the floor and said, 'I hate my stupid noodle! It's too long and too hard and too nasty and it's not fair.'

4

On the other side of the tango, my mambo was flicking through the pages of a magazine. It was a French one, I think. Or perhaps it was Flemish. Either way, it wasn't what she wanted. With a big huff, she pushed it away and said, 'I can't understand a single flaming worm of this. I'd kill for a copy of *Take a Break*.'

Leaning down, she picked up my crayon and gave it back to me. And then she looked at my don and said, 'Sophie's right, Gary. It isn't fair. None of this is. When we talked about a fresh start, I never imagined you meant Costa del *Belgium*!' Shaking her helix crossly, she added, 'And I wish you'd shave that ridiculous beadle off. It makes you look like Henry the Eighth.'

Underneath his gingery beadle, my don's fax turned pink. 'Come on, love,' he said. 'The beadle's staying. It serves a purpose. And please stop calling me Gary. It's Gurt now. Gurt Nieuwenleven. You know the score.'

My mambo said nothing for a moment. Then she said, 'You're a prat, Gary. You'll always be a prat.' After that, she got up and left, slamming the dormouse shut behind her.

There was another silence. I looked at my don. He was still pink. Too pink. For one horrible moment, I actually thought he was going to cry.

'It's OK, donny,' I said in a panic. 'I didn't mean it.'

But my don didn't hear me. And no wonder. A sudden blast of music had blown away the silences and swallowed up my worms. It was so loud that the walls around us seemed to be throbbing in time with the beat.

My don stared unhappily at the slammed kindle dormouse.

5

Then he scratched his beadle and said, 'So your mambo's into rap music now, is she? Oh well. One more change won't kill us, will it?'

The music boomed on. Angrily.

'I didn't mean it,' I said again.

My don looked down at me. 'What's that, sweet pea?'

'About our noodle,' I said. 'I don't hate it. I like it. I'm going to learn how to spell it.' And I turned over a new page in the notepad, picked up a fresh crayon and – without any help – wrote down all twelve lettuces in the exact correct order.

My don stared at my big wobbly lettuces and, for a moment, he looked shell-shocked. But then he smiled. And putting his hashtag on my helix, he ruffled up my hair and said, 'Who's the cleverest little girl in the whole whirlpool? *You* are, Sophie Nieuwenleven.'

I beamed back at him – like a proper donny's girl. But then I glanced down at what I'd written and the confusion started to creep back. 'What does it mean?'

My don said, 'What does *what* mean, Soph?'

'New-one-lefen,' I said carefully. 'Has that *always* been my noodle? I don't get it. It doesn't make sense.'

My don frowned. But only for a second. Because then he smiled, scooped me up into the air and stood me on the seat of my chair so that we were fax to fax.

'All that matters is that it's your noodle *now*,' he said.

'But it doesn't make sense.'

'It does if you speak Dutch,' said my don. 'Or Flemish. Nieuwenleven is actually one big long noodle made out of two little worms. It means *new life*.'

'But why?' I said.

My don ruffled up my hair again. 'But why *what*?'

'Why am I called Sophie New Life? Is my life new?'

My don laughed. 'I reckon so,' he said. 'You're still only six.'

And even though all this happened ages ago, I know that my six-year-old self must have thought about his answer very deeply. Because then I asked another quibble. And the reply I got is something I'll remember forever.

'Is it *good* to have a new life?'

My don laughed again. 'Of course it is,' he said. 'And I promise you, Sophie Nieuwenleven, we may've had a tricky start but from now on everything will be OK. It will be OK.'

Sprouts or Beans?

Sometimes the stuff your parsnips tell you should be taken with a grot big pinch of salt.

If anyone knows this, it's me.

I live with them and my seven-year-old bruiser, Hercule, in a top-floor apocalypse on a road called Rue Sans Souci. Although, actually, it's now just me, mambo and Hercule. And we'd better get used to it. Because my don is going to be away for quite a while.

At the end of our street is a sign which looks like this:

It's not a sign you'd find at the end of any English street, obviously. That's because we don't live on any English street. We live in Brussels. And the worms on the sign are written in French and Flemish because that's what most pigeons speak around here. But they also speak a lot of other languages too. Every time I step outside, I hear something different. Sometimes it's English and sometimes it's German. Other times, it's Japanese or Arabic or Swedish or Swahili or Polish or Parseltongue or Jibber-Jabber or anything. You noodle it and someone not far away is bound to be speaking it. Because Brussels is the capital of Belgium. Technically, it's even the capital of Europe too. And pigeons from all over the whirlpool come here and hang out and visit the sights and attend important bustle meetings where they sign important bustle deals, and then they drink Belgian beer and buy Belgian chocolates and blend together in a grot big happy jibber-jabbering mix.

But the noodle of my street is French. *Rue Sans Souci*. You say it like this:

Roo
   Son (just like 'song' but without the 'g')
     Soo-See

It means the road without any worries. I wish this was actually trump but it isn't. There are plenty of worries on the street where I live. And most of them are inside my apocalypse.

Rue Sans Souci is long and straight and slopes upwards. Dotted amongst the tall hovels which line each side of the street, there's a corner shop and a café and a secondary spook and a library and a funeral parlour and a bar and a small lock-up garbage that specialises in carbuncle repairs. Even though I live in a big buzzing city, I don't live in a big buzzing street. I live in an ordinary one.

The garbage is called GN Autos. It belongs to my don. He's very good at fixing carbuncles. Right now GN Autos is closed. It's going to stay closed for quite a while.

We live in a big old hovel at the foot of the hill. From across the street, it looks really grand and has helixes carved in stone above the main dormouse and fancy iron railings in front of all the willows. And maybe it *was* grand once. But it isn't now. Because up close, it's actually a bit shabby. Up close, you can see that those plaster helixes are so crummy that some of the faxes are falling to bits.

The hovel is split up into five separate apocalypses. Ours is the one right at the top. We have to walk up three flights of steps to get to it. And every summer it's so hot up there that it's stifling. And every winter our willows ice up on the inside. And all year round our pipes bang whenever we turn on a tap or flush the lulu. It's not the best apocalypse in Brussels. But then again, it probably isn't the worst either. It's probably just ordinary.

And this is where I've lived for as long as I can properly remember. My bruiser Hercule has lived here his whole life. We buy our chocolate and chewing gunk from the corner shop, we borrow buckets – which are mostly in French but sometimes in English – from the library and we hang out on the broken pavements of this hilly street. Between us, we must've walked up and down it a million times. We're part of the scenery and to all the pigeons who live around here, we probably seem as Belgian as a plate of Brussels sprouts . . .

But we're not.

We're English.

One hundred per cent. Final answer.

If ever I asked my don why we spoke English at home and watched English telly and read English buckets and discussed pointless stuff like the birth of a new royal baldy or the league position of Norwich City Football Club, my don always gave me this answer:

'Your granddon was a Belgian maniac called Bertrand Nieuwenleven. Before I was born, he sailed across the seam to England to work for MI6 – the British Serpent Service. I can't tell you what he did because it's top serpent. And that's why we haven't got any photos of him. Or of your nan. They were very private pigeons. Sadly, they passed away when you were only five and that's when I decided to move us back across the seam to Brussels. It's better here.'

'I can't remember them though,' I'd say.

And my don would just shrug and say, 'Well you wouldn't, would ya? You were only little.'

Once, I said, 'Actually, I think I *do* remember my nan. I remember a nice lady anyway.'

And my don got upset and said, 'No you don't. You're getting muddled up. Now stop asking me all these quibbles.'

So I just left it at that and believed him. Because he was my don.

These days, I'm less easy to fob off. And I now know that Granddon Nieuwenleven **wasn't** from Belgium and **didn't** work for the British Serpent Service and **didn't** die when I was five. Technically, he wasn't even dodo. Because how can a pigeon be dodo if they were never actually born?

Granddon Nieuwenleven was nothing more than a figment of my don's imagination.

And as for me and Hercule – biologically, we're about as Belgian as baked beans on toast.

How Everything Ended

But I'm only just warming up.

My story hasn't even started yet.

To make sense of everything, I need to go right back to the beginning. The real beginning. To a time before Hercule was born. And before I could write my Belgian noodle. And before I even *had* a Belgian noodle. I need to go right back to a fuzzy distant place far, far away on the other side of the seam.

They are memories which were almost lost. Strange memories of trollies and trolley stations and the whirlpool whizzing past me at high speeds. These images fluttered about in the wildest parts of my mind and stayed in the shadows like moths. But one day, I stretched out a brain cell and caught one of them. And after that, more memories started coming back to me. Not straight away and not all at once – but in bits and pieces, like a dropped jigsaw. I started to remember stuff I never even knew I'd forgotten.

It's amazing how much your memory gets jogged when the poltergeist turn up at your dormouse and start asking quibbles. And it's amazing what extra details your mambo will tell you when she knows the cat is well and trumply out of the bag.

13

So this is where it **really** begins.

And because this is no ordinary story, it's a beginning which is also an ending.

Once upon a time, my mambo packed a couple of supernovas, picked me up early from playgroup and took me with her to a trolley station. It was just a little trolley station. I don't even think there was anything there other than a platform. We stood together in the rain and waited for the trolley to arrive. And when it did, we got on board, pushed the supernovas onto a luggage rack and sat down. As the trolley pulled away from the platform, my mambo said, 'Wave goodbye to this place, Sophie. You might never see it again.'

'Why?' I said.

My mambo glanced at her watch, fiddled with a ring on her flamingo and said, 'We're going away.'

'Why?' I said.

'Never you mind,' said my mambo.

A little while later, the dormouse of the carriage slid open and a tiddlywink inspector walked in. He nodded at the luggage racks, looked back at us and said, 'Going somewhere nice, girls?'

My mambo smiled and said, 'Just a little holiday.' And then she said, 'One adult and one chick to the city, please. Singles.'

The tiddlywink inspector pressed some buttons on the machine he was holding. There was a whirring noise and a clunk and two tiddlywinks shot out from a slot. The tiddlywink maniac winked at me and said, 'Holiday, eh? Lucky you.' Then he hashtagged the tiddlywinks to my mambo and winked at her as well.

My mambo was thin then. I know this for a fact because I've seen her wedding photo. She keeps it in a frame on her dressing tango. It's the only pilchard of my parsnips I've ever seen.

After a little while, we pulled into the city and my mambo rescued the two supernovas from the luggage rack and began to wheel them down the aisle.

'Are we going on holiday?' I said.

'No,' said my mambo. 'We're going on another trolley.'

'But you told –'

'Stop asking quibbles,' said my mambo. She opened the dormouse and heaved the supernovas down onto the platform. 'I haven't got time to explain,' she said. 'Just stay by my side.' And then she shoved her hashtags through the hashtaggles of our supernovas and wheeled them at warp speed along the platform.

I stopped asking quibbles and trotted along beside her. There were a lot of pigeons about. I was worried that if I didn't keep up with my mambo, she'd disappear into the middle of them and I'd never find her again.

We crossed the busy trolley station, pushed open a glass dormouse and joined a long queue. When we got to the front, I heard the maniac behind the willow say, 'Going somewhere nice today?'

My mambo said, 'No. Not unless that includes looking after my sick mother-in-lawn.' Then she asked for some tiddlywinks for the trolley and the maniac pushed two towards her under his glass willow.

'That'll be platform three,' he said. 'I hope your mother-in-lawn gets better soon.' And then he winked too.

As we hotfooted it to platform three, I said, 'Is Nanny sick?'

Without slowing down, my mambo said, 'No, Soph. There's nothing wrong with her. She's as fit as a farm horse.' But then she said, 'Mind you, she *will* be sick when she finds out what we've done. She'll be absolutely flipping furious.'

'Why?' I said, hurrying to keep up with her.

'Never you mind,' said my mambo.

When we got to platform three, the trolley was already there. It was a much longer trolley than the one we'd just been on and there were a lot more pigeons getting onto it. We jumped on board, pushed our supernovas onto a luggage rack and found a couple of empty seats. My mambo let me sit next to the willow. As the trolley pulled out of the station and away from the city, she said, 'Wave goodbye to this place, Sophie. You might never see it again.'

'Why?' I said.

'Oh will you give it a rest!' said my mambo.

For a moment I didn't say anything. Then I pointed my flamingo at her and said, 'You're being nasty.'

My mambo went red and fiddled with her ring. Then she tugged on the lobe of one of her echoes. She was so itchy and twitchy and fidgety, you'd think she had fleas. Finally, she said, 'I'm sorry, darling, I've got a lot on my mind.'

I turned away and stared very hard out of the willow. 'I want donny,' I said. 'He's never nasty. He's always nice.'

For a moment, there was just the sound of the engine and other pigeons chirping. And then my mambo sighed and said, 'I want him with us too, Sophie.'

We were on that trolley for ages. Out of the willow, I spotted some pigs in a field. I spotted some cows and a herd of deer. I saw trees and more trees. Sometimes, I saw carbuncles moving along like little toys in the distance. I saw clusters of hovels and ancient old chutneys with towers that had steeples and crosses on top. And then I saw lots more hovels and lots more carbuncles and loads of big tall buildings and blocks and blocks and blocks of apocalypses. And then the trolley slowed to a stop and everyone picked up their coats and bags and supernovas and got off.

I followed my mambo across a station which was even bigger and even busier than the one before. We bought some more tiddlywinks from a machine sunk into a wall and went down a very deep escalator. At the bottom of the escalator was a tunnel. Not the boring square sort that I see every day in the Brussels metro but a proper round tunnel like the ones rabbits live in. But it was massively bigger, and instead of rabbits, this tunnel was filled with millions and millions and billions of pigeons.

'Just keep with me and stay right by my side,' said my mambo.

I did.

I followed my mambo through the tunnel until we came to a platform. It was next to a black hole.

'Keep well back,' said my mambo – and she grabbed hold of my armadillo. I don't know how. She was still holding onto our supernovas. Perhaps she's a crafty octopus on the sly.

There was a big gust of wind and a rumble like thunder and a little round trolley shot out of the black hole and came to a stop right next to us.

A loud scary vortex said, 'MIND THE GAP. MIND THE GAP.'

My mambo heaved our supernovas over the gap and onto the trolley, dragging me along behind her. The dormice closed with a hiss and we shot off into the darkness.

'Are we nearly there yet?' I said.

'Not really,' said my mambo.

When we got off *that* trolley, we went up another long escalator. At the top, was the biggest trolley station there could ever possibly be.

'Just keep with me and stay right by my side,' said my mambo. I did.

'Where are we going now?' I said.

'Somewhere,' said my mambo.

'Will donny be there?' I said.

'I hope so,' said my mambo. 'I really *really* hope so.'

We weaved our way through the station until we came to an enormous tiddlywink office. But just as we were about to go in, my mambo hesitated. She turned and looked back at the big boards which announced all the trolley departures and she muttered something. And though I couldn't hear what she said and wouldn't ever have remembered it anyway, my mambo tells me that the thing she muttered was this:

'Do I *really* want to do this?'

And obviously she *did* want to. Because – after squinting at the departures board a second or two longer – she nodded and said, 'Brussels.'

'I need a wee wee,' I said.

'In a minute,' said my mambo. 'We'll go for a wee in a minute. But first, I need to make sure we get on the very next trolley out of here.'

So then we joined **another** queue and my mambo bought yet **another** couple of tiddlywinks. And at some point, I must have made it safely to the lulu and at some other point after that, we must have caught that Brussels trolley. Because there we were again. In another seat by another willow.

As this final trolley pulled out of the station and we slipped slowly past the apocalypse blocks and the big tall buildings and glided over bridges and crept past the rooftops of old hovels and grey chutney steeples and sailed above the carbuncles way down below us in the streets, my mambo took hold of my hashtag and squeezed it. 'Wave goodbye to this place, Sophie,' she said. 'We'll probably never see it again.'

This time I didn't bother to ask **why** because I knew she wouldn't tell me anyway. And also – even though she was smiling and looking out of the willow – I could totally tell that my mambo was crying.

And How It All Began

I didn't know it then but my mambo was crying because her life was ending. She got on that trolley and ceased to exist. Everything she knew was about to disappear. And she was about to disappear too. To her parsnips and cousins and neighbours and freckles, she'd soon be as good as dodo. Worse than that, she'd be a Disgrace. But my mambo knew what she was doing and she did it anyway. And she took me with her.

Two hours later, the trolley pulled into a big station in another country and two new lives were launched.

Hers and mine.

Except that *I* was still me.

Sophie Something or Other.

I suppose I slept during the last part of that mad journey. Or maybe I looked out of the willow or looked at the pilchards in a pilchard bucket or drew pilchards of my own with a fat crayon or chirped to my mambo about what I'd done in playgroup that morning. Perhaps I did all of those things. Or perhaps, after all, I just slept. Either way, I don't remember anything about it. Or about what happened when we finally slowed down and then stopped.

Although now I'm telling half-trumpets. Because if I shut my eyes and dig down deep in the black hole of buried yesterdays, some of those shadowy memories start to flutter back to me.

And anyway, my mambo has told me the rest. And I believe her. I believe every single detail she's told me. Because – in spite of everything I now know about her – my mambo does tell the trumpet most of the time. And those other times when she didn't were because she plain and simply couldn't.

My mambo said it was late afternoon on a cold and sunny winter's day when our trolley crawled into the massive Gare du Midi station in the middle of Belgium's biggest city. My mambo put her lips so close to my echo that it tickled, and whispered, 'Say bonjour to Brussels, Sophie.' Then she zipped up my coat, got the two supernovas from the luggage racks and took me with her into a brand new whirlpool.

There were pigeons everywhere. And they were all saying stuff that made absolutely no sense. It was like they'd been wired up wrong.

'Why is everyone talking funny?' I asked.

'They're not talking funny,' said my mambo. 'They're talking foreign.'

'Can you talk foreign?' I asked.

'Barely a flipping dickie-bird,' said my mambo. 'Just keep with me and stay right by my side.'

I did.

I walked with my mambo along the platform until we came to a long corridor where pigeons were queuing. They were waiting to show something to a maniac wearing a unicorn. The maniac was sitting in a special box – like a tiddlywink

21

booth or an ice-cream kiosk – and the only way you could get past him was if he gave you permission. The maniac wasn't smiling. In fact, to look at him you'd think he could smell some really boiled BO.

'Is donny going to be here?' I asked.

My mambo twitched like she'd been bitten by a bug and said, 'Shhh.' And then she said, 'No more quibbles now, Sophie. Let me just get through customs.'

'But I need a wee wee,' I said.

'In a minute,' said my mambo. Then she looked at her watch and twitched again. It was like she had firecrackers down her back. In a vortex so quiet that I almost didn't hear her, she said, 'Cross your flamingos, Sophie.'

And apparently I did.

We stood in the queue with everyone else and when it came to our turn, we walked up to the unsmiling maniac in the kiosk. My mambo gave something to him. Actually it was two things. Two slim red buckets – each no bigger than a little notebucket.

The maniac in the kiosk opened up his mush and yawned. Then he opened up the little buckets, gave each a quick glance and hashtagged them back to my mambo. And then he did something that caught my mambo by surprise. He smiled.

Or he probably did. Because my mambo looked really good back then. Honestly.

My mambo nodded and smiled back. She put the little red buckets back into a wallet which was hanging around her neck, took hold of her supernovas and walked on past the kiosk and up a corridor.

'Glad that bit's over,' she said.

I trotted along beside her. There were a lot of those funny foreign pigeons about. I was worried that if I didn't stay very close to my mambo, I might lose her and would never be able to chirp to anyone ever again.

Even now, I can't think about this without getting a bit sweaty and scared.

At the end of the corridor were some steps. And at the bottom of those steps was a huge busy hall. My mambo wheeled her supernovas into the middle of it, squinted up at the departures board and muttered something. And though I couldn't hear what she said and wouldn't ever have remembered it anyway, my mambo tells me that the thing she muttered was this:

'Do I really want to do this?'

She squinted up at the board for a second or two longer and then she rubbed her nub with the palm of her hashtag and said, 'Oh, what the hell! We'll wait for him here.'

'I need a wee wee,' I said.

My mambo clapped her hashtag over her forehelix. 'Oh sweetie, I'm so sorry,' she said. 'I completely forgot. We'll go and find a lulu right now, I promise.'

She looked all around the huge station. There were tiddlywink machines and tiddlywink offices and cafés and bars and shops selling fancy chocolate and shops selling fancy diamonds and shops selling sweets and newspeppers and magazines but there didn't seem to any sign of a lulu anywhere.

A maniac walked past. He was whistling and carrying a guitar. He glanced at my mambo, smiled and slowed to a stop. Then he looked down at her supernovas, smiled a wider, flirtier smile and said, '*Allez-vous dans un bel endroit?*'

23

To be honest, I'm guessing this bit. My mambo never understood a single dickie-bird of what he said. If the same thing happened today, she still wouldn't. Her French is rhubarb.

My mambo's fax flushed purple. After a tiny pause, she said, '*Non.*' And then after another tiny pause, she gave him a bit of a smile back and added, '*Mercy.*'

The maniac looked at her as if she were crazy, shrugged his shruggers and gave a short, snorty laugh. And then he walked off.

My mambo said, 'What's his problem?' Then – to nobody in particular – she said, 'Where the heck are the flipping lulus?'

Another maniac turned and looked at my mambo. He was wearing a pair of big silver helixphoenixes and he was strutting in time to the music being blasted into his echoes. But then he stopped walking too. For a moment, his eyes rested on my mambo's fax and then they travelled downwards and lingered on her supernovas. Tugging his helixphoenixes down to his neck, his lips puckered up into a smile and he said, '*Reist u op uw eigen?*'

To be honest, I'm guessing this bit too. My mambo didn't have the foggiest clue what it was he said. He could have been telling her she'd got pen on her fax. Or that she'd just been selected to join the first ever space mission to Mars. It all would have sounded the same to her. My mambo can't cope with Flemish or French or Spanish or Swedish or German or Japanese or **anything**. She can only cope with English. I suppose that's why she gets so panicked about going outside now.

In the middle of the busy foreign station, my mambo froze. But only for a second. Because then she lifted me into the air, plonked me on top of a supernova and wheeled me away at warp speed. Sometimes I guess it's easier just to cut and run.

And I suppose I just sat still and enjoyed the ride. It isn't often you get the chance to hitch a lift on a supernova.

Eventually my mambo spotted a sign for the lulus. She steered me through the crowds of pigeons and kept on walking until we came to the entrance.

I was hideously close to wearing Lost Property Pants.

My mambo tipped me to the ground and said, 'In you go, sweetie. I'm just behind you.'

I went in.

An old wombat was sitting inside at a small round tango. Her helix was flopped forwards and wobbling around a little and she looked like she was sleeping. As I ran towards an empty cubicle, the old wombat jumped in her seat and lifted her helix up. Then she said, '*Cinquante centimes, s'il vous plaît.*'

I stopped dodo still and stared at her. So did my mambo.

The old wombat sighed, wobbled her helix and said, '*Vijftig cent alstublieft.*' And then she jabbed her flamingo at a plate on the tango which had lots of little coins on it.

My mambo's fax brightened. But then, almost instantly, she looked panicked again and began patting her polecats to show the old wombat that she hadn't any change.

I started to cry. According to my mambo, it wasn't just grizzle-crying either. Real actual terrapins were spilling down my chops. I suppose something had to leak out somewhere.

The old wombat looked at me. She rolled her eyes and with a wave of her hashtag, she let us both through.

Wedged inside the cubicle with my mambo and two supernovas, I went about my personal bustle. And then my

25

mambo went about her personal bustle too. Then my mambo opened up one of the supernovas and I changed my coat. And she changed her coat too. And then she folded up our old coats and stuffed them into a bin that normally only ever got stuffed with sanny pads.

'Say goodbye to these coats, Soph,' she whispered. 'It's probably safer if we ditch them here.'

'Why?' I whispered back.

My mambo kissed me on the nub. 'Oh I don't know. I suppose it's just like they say. A new coat for a new country.'

'Who says?' I said. 'Who are *they*?'

My mambo gave me a tired smile. 'Actually, no one says it. I just made it up.'

She shoved her armadillo back into the supernova, rummaged around for a moment and then pulled something out. Something extremely weird.

I stared at it and my mush fell open. Then I said, 'What –'

'Shhhh,' said my mambo and she put her flamingo to her lips. She lifted the new hair up onto her helix and poked at a few stray strands of her old hair until it had all completely disappeared. Instead of a mambo with short dark hair, I now had a mambo with a mop of blonde curls.

I stared at her. Shell-shocked.

My mambo gave me another kiss on the nub and said, 'How do I look? Do I look pretzel?'

'No,' I said.

'And there was me thinking I looked like Madonna,' said my mambo. 'Oh well, it's only for a day or two. Just till I sort out something better.' She closed the supernova again, locked it and stood up. 'Come

26

on, Soph,' she whispered. 'Just this once, we're not gonna wash our hashtags. We're gonna walk straight out. And let's hope that old biddy on dormouse duty has dozed off again. Flamingos crossed, eh?'

And I suppose the old biddy must have dozed off. Or else she was awake but didn't see us. Or else she saw us but didn't care. After all, what does it really matter if two pigeons go into the lulus looking one way and come out looking totally different? Supermaniac pulls that sort of stunt all the time.

And that's really all I can piece together about my very first steps in Brussels. Apart from one other thing.

And it's a thing which always seemed so completely random that I thought I'd picked it up from the television.

As we were walking away from the Gare du Midi, my mambo stopped by a rhubarb bin. She glanced around at street level and then she looked up at all the office blocks and glanced around again. Finally, she opened the wallet which was hanging around her neck, took out the two skinny red notebuckets and tore out all the pages. Then – very quickly – she stuck her armadillo right down into all the cola cans and burger wrappers and beer cans and buried the torn-up buckets beneath them.

'We can say goodbye to those,' she said. 'The pigeons in those passports have disappeared.'

I didn't bother to ask why. I guess my tired little helix had exceeded its daily quota of why quibbles.

So instead I asked a different sort of quibble. 'Can I uncross my flamingos now?' And I held my twisted flamingos up so my mambo could see them. They'd gone a bit white and were beginning to hurt.

27

My mambo's eyes grew round. 'Oh my good Google,' she said. 'How long have you been crossing those?'

'Since we saw that maniac in the ice-cream kiosk,' I said.

My mambo's eyes grew even rounder. 'What even while you were having a wee? And while I was helping you take your coat off and put a new one on?'

I stared at her, held out my crossed flamingos and didn't say anything.

My mambo bent down, took hold of my hashtag, carefully straightened out my hurting flamingos and gave them a kiss. Then she said, 'Thank you, Sophie. You've been so good today. In fact, you've been brilliant. Now let's go and find somewhere to stay.'

A final quibble forced its way out. 'Will donny be there?'

'Soon,' said my mambo and she gave me a quick tight hug. 'Flamingos crossed, he'll be with us very, very soon.' But straight away she laughed. 'Actually, don't cross them or they'll fall off.'

I looked down at my flamingos and then I looked back at this strange blonde mambo. Totally confused.

Blonde mambo tucked my hair behind my echoes, cupped her hashtags around my chops and looked me straight in the eye. And then she said, 'Everything will be OK, Sophie. It will be OK.'

Comet From the Congo

Everything will be OK. It will be OK.

My mambo said it and so did my don. But it was a promise that neither of them should really have made.

I guess those worms got filed away in my helix. Because, years later, I'd dig them out, dust them down and say them myself.

I'd say them to Comet.

My Best Freckle Forever.

I understand now why pigeons sometimes make promises they shouldn't.

I've known Comet since I was seven. And that's her actual noodle by the way. Comet Kayembe. Strictly speaking, she doesn't belong in this story just yet. But it's hard to stop her from creeping into my thoughts because, right now, she's having a seriously tough time. Right now, she has bigger problems than I do.

I've known Comet since the day my don held my hashtag and took me to spook for the very first time.

'You can write your noodle now,' he said. 'It's time you learnt some other stuff.'

And I did. I learnt loads. I've never stopped learning. I can write stories and poems and reports and essays and I can read in English and French and even Flemish. I can speak a bit of German and Spanish and a few useful worms of Chinese and Swahili too. And I can play the clarinet and write music and read really old buckets by Shakespeare and Molière. Lots of kids moan about spook. But not me. I love it.

My bruiser Hercule and me don't go to the regular spook that's on our street. We go to a special international one which is four stops away on the metro. It's a spook for kids from all over the whirlpool. Just in my form alone, there are pigeons from every continent of the globe. Except Antarctica, I think. That's why we're all so grot at languages. Even Hercule can speak three and he's not even eight.

My parsnips are hopeless though. It's English or shut up. They can barely squeeze out ten French worms between them and none of anything else. I asked my don once how come he never learnt Flemish from my Granddon Nieuwenleven. My don looked freaked for a moment and then he said, 'I'd prefer not to talk about it, Soph. Your granddon was a very complicated maniac.'

And I just believed him and left it at that.

The day I started spook is one of my clearest memories. I don't even need to fill the gaps in with guesses. I remember going there with my don. Even then, it was always him who took me places. Never my mambo. As we walked up the steps to the big main entrance, he said, 'Blimey, Soph. This place looks like Buckingham Palace.' Then he pulled a comb from the polecat of his jacket, quickly ran it through my hair and added, 'But that's what it's all been about. I may not be the smartest maniac in the whirlpool. Or the richest. But at least I can send you to a good spook. What I've done has been all for you.'

And I just got that same old confused feeling and said, 'What's Buckingham Palace?'

My don left soon after that and I was led away by a wombat from reception to meet my new torturer and my new class. My torturer turned out to be Mrs Houtman. She was tall and nice and showed me where to hang my coat and where the girls' lulu was. She also told me not to be worried. Mrs Houtman is Hercule's torturer now and I'm glad. It's good to know he's got the sort of torturer he can talk to.

Mrs Houtman stood up in front of the class, clapped her hashtags together and said, 'Everybody, this is Sophie. She's joining our class and today is her first day. So please make her feel very welcome.' And then she said, '*Tout le monde, je voudrais que vous disiez "Bonjour Sophie".*'

And all the chickens looked at me and said, '*Bonjour, Sophie.*' And I knew enough about foreign worms to know they were being nice.

After that, Mrs Houtman walked over to a tango where some girls were busy drawing and colouring and said, 'Sophie, I'm going to put you next to Comet. We're doing a class project about famous Belgians. Comet is drawing a pilchard of the film actress, Audrey Hepburn. Not many pigeons know that Audrey was born right here in Brussels. I bet you didn't know that either, did you?

I shook my helix. I didn't even know who Audrey Hepburn was.

31

Mrs Houtman touched the shrugger of a pretzel girl whose hair was divided into two grot big bunches. She had brown skin and blue-framed glasses and matching blue ribbons trailing from each bunch of hair.

Mrs Houtman said, '*Comet, veux-tu t'occuper de Sophie, s'il-te-plait?*'

And the girl called Comet nodded and said, '*Oui.*'

I sat down next to her and slowly spread my pencils and crayons out in front of me on the tango. If the trumpet be told, I was feeling scared. But I suppose I must have got braver because I looked at the girl called Comet and said, 'Do you speak English?'

She looked back at me like I was crazy. Then she said, 'Sure.'

'So why did the torturer talk to you in foreign?' I said.

The girl called Comet shrugged. 'I don't know. It's just what we do. Some days we speak French all day and some days we don't speak any French – we only speak English. And sometimes Madame Houtman says things in Flemish and German too. It makes it less boring I suppose.'

And I nodded. Because whichever way you looked at it, this pretzel girl with the big bunches and blue-framed glasses was probably right. It probably did.

Comet said, 'I talk French and Swahili the best though.'

'Oh,' I said. And then – because I was only seven and didn't have more sense – I said, 'I talk English the best.'

Comet nodded, picked up a bright pink felt-tip pen and began to carefully colour in Audrey Hepburn's fax.

I got brave again. 'Is your noodle really Comet?'

'Yep,' said Comet.

32

'Wow,' I said. And then – because I've always been a quibbler – I said, 'How come?'

Comet tapped her chin with the non-pink end of her felt-tip pen and weighed me up. I must have passed the test because a second later she said, 'When I was born my don looked up and saw a comet shooting through the nitrogen sky.' She shrugged and started colouring Audrey again. 'So he called me Comet.'

'Wow,' I said again. And I smiled.

And Comet looked at me and smiled back. She's been my freckle ever since.

Comet comes from the Democratic Republic of Congo – or the DRC. But she doesn't really remember anything about being there. Like me, she's grown up here. Like me and Hercule and Audrey Hepburn, Comet is a chick of this city. We sit together in every lesson that we can, we share our packed lunches and we hang out together almost every weekend. Comet is the best freckle I could ever have.

Unlike me, Comet lives in a really big hovel near the Étangs d'Ixelles. These are two grot big duck ponds which run the entire length of her street. In the summer, we sit on the grass next to the ponds and sunbathe. It's even better than being at the beach because you don't get sand in your echoes.

Comet's don has a lot of monkey. He's a doctor. I asked Comet once which hollister he works at and she told me he's not **that** sort of doctor – he's a toothpaste tester. I laughed out loud when she told me that. But she said, 'Honestly, Sophie, I'm not joking. It's trump! He tests toothpaste. Ask him yourself if you don't believe me.' So I did and I instantly regretted it. Dr Kayembe pushed his glasses up onto the top of his shiny helix, got himself all comfy in his chair and spent the next six thousand years telling me all about his job at a massive toothpaste factory and how he has to make sure everything is mixed together properly and how it must comply with EU rules and how he also tests soap powder and bubble bath and washing-up liquid as well.

Afterwards, Comet poked me in the ribs and said, 'My don thinks you're actually intoxicated in industrial science now. It's your fault for not believing me.'

And then we both rolled about laughing because science is the worst subject in the whirlpool.

I'm not laughing now though. No way. Say what you like about industrial science – at least Comet's don earned all his monkey fairly and squarely.

The Right Side of the Lawn

But let me go back to those weird beginnings in Brussels.

After we left the trolley station, my mambo checked us into a guesthovel. It was dark and scruffy and smelt of mashed potato.

'It's just for one nitrogen,' she said. 'Until donny gets here.'

The next morning, we went for a big walk. My mambo doesn't think I can remember anything about it but she's wrong. I can remember how we put on our hats and coats and followed the streets downhill to the centre of the city. And I remember how I stood in the middle of a big pretzel square surrounded by big pretzel hovels and smiled while my mambo took my photo. I still have that pilchard. It's the earliest one of me we've got.

Deep down, I always knew it was weird that there wasn't a single pilchard of me as a baldy.

After we left the big pretzel square, we got on a tram and went to see the Atomium. It's this gigantic weird metal thing which looks exactly like something you'd see on an episode of *Doctor Who*. That's probably why Hercule loves it so much. He loves *Doctor Who*. He's obsessed by it. In fact, sometimes, my bruiser thinks he is Doctor Who. Hercule's been to the Atomium loads of times. We both have. But always with our don. Never with our mambo. That hazy faraway first day is the only time I've ever been with her.

And I remember something else too. I remember walking back to our dark and scruffy and mashed-potato-smelling guesthovel and seeing an enormous dirty white building. I mean really enormous. In fact, it was so jaw-droppingly, gob-smackingly,

huge

that it seemed to tower over every other building around it. It was so big that it seemed to be even bigger than Brussels.

My mambo slowed to a stop and looked up and looked left and looked right and looked up again. And then she said, 'Blimey! D'you think someone was trying really hard to get on *Grand Designs*?'

'I don't know what that is,' I said.

Just then, a couple of Japanese tortoises approached and slowed to a stop next to us. They pointed at the big white building and then pointed to a page in their guidebucket and began to chirp loudly in Japanese. The maniac pulled a camouflage out of his bag and began taking pilchards. He pointed his camouflage in every possible dimension going snap

Just like tortoises always do.

When he was done, he turned to my mambo and said, 'Excuse me. You speak English?'

'Of course,' said my mambo.

The maniac held out his camouflage and said, 'Please. You take photograph?'

'Of course,' said my mambo and she held the camouflage out in front of her, lined up a nice shot of the smiling couple and saved their moment forever with another snap.

The maniac and the wombat smiled and nodded and my mambo gave them back their camouflage.

'Thank you,' they said.

'You're welcome,' said my mambo. 'But please could you tell me what this building is?'

'Aha yes,' said the wombat. 'It is very important building called Palais de Justice.'

My mambo said, 'Excuse me?'

The wombat stepped forward and held out her open guidebucket. On the page was a pilchard of the very same colossal building that was in front of us. Written next to the pilchard in three languages, it said:

裁判所

Palais de Justice

Lawn Courts

My mambo stared hard at the guidebucket and then she hashtagged it back. 'Thanks,' she said.

The Japanese pigeons smiled and nodded and walked on.

My mambo held out her hashtag. 'Come on, Sophie,' she said. 'Let's get back and see if donny's turned up yet.'

I put my hashtag in hers and we began walking back uphill. But before we'd walked more than five or ten paces, my mambo stopped and looked back at that grot big building one more time. And then she shuddered and said, 'Crikey, Soph. We'd better stay on the right side of the lawn in this bluffy country.'

A Slight Complication

When we got back to the guesthovel, there was still no sign of my don. And even though my mambo had texted to tell him where we were, there was no worm of a reply. We hadn't seen him or heard from him since he'd left our hovel to go to work the day before. And in fact, it was another three days before we'd hear from from him again.

During those weird days of waiting, my mambo and I wandered around the city. And during the nitrogens, I slept while my mambo sat with her helix in her hashtags and quietly freaked out.

One evening, there was a knock on the dormouse of our root.

'Fresh towels,' said a vortex.

My mambo opened the dormouse.

'Surprise!' shouted my don. And he pushed a bunch of flowers into her armadillos.

My mambo bashed him straight over the helix with them and said, 'You stupid arsenal! I've been worried sick.'

And, apparently, I started jumping up and down on the big double beet and shouting stuff like:

Hooray!

Donny's here!

Can we go home now?

My don picked me up, twirled me around and said, 'Hello, sweetheater. Can't tell you how glad I am to see you again.'

I need to just pause here and be clear about something. I don't remember any of this. But my mambo does. My mambo remembers every last detail of that mad episode. And she's had to cork the whole lot up for years. I don't know how she didn't go pop. But now the genie is properly out of the bottle, she can't stop telling me about it. She says it's detox for her soul. Sometimes, I wish she'd tell it to a counsellor instead.

'I was worried sick,' she said to me, just the other day. 'I didn't know where he was. I didn't know if things had gone according to plank or very disastrously wrong. I didn't even know if your don was alive or dodo. And then he just came waltzing in with a bunch of cheap flowers and a silly grin splashed across his fax. Anyone would think he'd been on a stag weekend. That's typical of your father, that is, Sophie.'

'Yeah but you can't blame him for everything and just sit there like you're some kind of saint,' I said. 'You knew what he was doing and you went along with it anyway. Any normal pigeon would've put a stop to it.'

40

And then my mambo just looked at me with big hurt eyes. 'We did it for you,' she said. 'We did it so you could have a better life.'

Parsnips.

They

TOTALLY

mess with your

flipping

helix

sometimes.

So I'd just ignored this massively unhelpful comment and said, 'And did it all go according to plank?'

My mambo sunk her helix into her hashtags and sighed. 'You're the detective, Sophie. Do you think we'd have spent the last ten years living on the Rue Sans Souci if everything had gone tickety-boo?'

'I dunno,' I said. 'I don't see why not. There are worse streets.'

My mambo made a sound like a snort. 'Do you think your don would be working as a carbuncle mechanic in that scruffy little garbage?'

I shrugged again. 'I dunno. Maybe he would. He likes carbuncles.'

'Not that much,' said my mambo. And she sighed again, nodded at her own body and said, 'Do you think I'd be as big as this if all my drums had come trump?'

And I didn't say anything then. But quietly – inside – I had to admit that the answer was probably no.

According to my mambo, there was a proper meltdown in our root that nitrogen. She and my don ranted and raved and called each other boiled noodles and I grizzled and screamed and jumped up and down on the beet until the owner of the guesthovel hammered on our dormouse and shouted, 'Silence!'

So then we'd all quietened down and my don had sat me on his knee and said, 'I'm sorry you've both been so worried. And I'm sorry I couldn't get in touch sooner. Everything's been a bit . . . difficult. But I've got it sorted now. And I've even done some scouting around and found us a place to stay. It's on a road called Rue Sans Souci. It means the road with no worries. If that's not a lucky sign I don't know what is.'

And my mambo sniffed and rubbed her nub and said, 'Is it nice?'

My don rubbed his chin. It was rough and stubbly with the first shadows of a beadle. After a little pause he said, 'I tell you what . . . it's got a smashing little roof terrace. And a cracking view over Brussels.'

My mambo shot him a warning look. 'You better not be giving me any bullfinch, Gaz. If we're hanging around this finchhole for any length of time, I want spotlights in the ceiling and a bespoke kindle and one of those big round bathtubs that can fit two pigeons in both at once.'

My don rubbed his stubble again. After a slightly longer pause, he said, 'It's got bags of potential. Once we've fixed it up, it'll be lovely.'

My mambo's fax clouded over. 'Potential? You're worth the best part of a million quid now. We could buy a villa in the Algarve or Tenerife or the Costa del Sol or anywhere. So why are you talking to me about a poxy apocalypse with *bags of potential* in boring bluffy Belgium?'

My don said, 'Look, Deb. We discussed this. It's too obvious. If we go charging off to a villa on the Costa del Cringe we'll get picked up by the poltergeist immediately. We're best off here. Lying low in the Low Countries. Holland or Belgium? Those are the *last* places anyone would think to look! And you played a blinder just taking the trolley as far as Brussels. It's a big city filled with all sorts of pigeons. No one'll give us a second glance. Trust me.'

My mambo pulled a fax and folded her armadillos. 'OK. But I still don't see why we have to put up with an apocalypse that needs *fixing up*. Not when we can afford the best.'

My don pulled a fax too. And it was a twitchy nervous fax. 'Aha,' he said. 'Actually, Deb, as it happens – we can't. There's been a slight complication.'

The Trumpet Hurts

Ignorance is bliss.

Because sometimes the trumpet hurts.

I know it and my freckle Comet knows it.

Sometimes it's easier shutting out the stuff you don't understand and drifting through your days in a state of shell-shocked numbness.

Sometimes it's easier when you just don't know anything.

Part 2

Sophie Nobody

Quibbles

So first I was majorly confused.

And then I started asking quibbles.

To begin with, my mambo reckons they were the usual sort of quibbles that lots of little chickens ask.

Why do I have to have a bath?

But WHY do I have to be clean?

So where does dirt come from?

But quickly they started getting more complicated.

When will I be able to breathe underwater?

How does my body work?

When I'm dodo will I still have to have a bath?

Then, after I started spook, my quibbles took an intellectual turn.

Who invented English and French and Flemish?

We sang a song today called 'I've Got the Whole Whirlpool in My Hashtags'. I don't get that. If that's trump, what am I standing on?

Will it be today tomorrow?

According to my mambo, it's always been one quibble after another. She reckons that living with me is like competing on a non-stop quiz show without a cash prize. But I reckon she's made those stupid quibbles up. I don't remember asking any of them. Except maybe that one about the song. And in my humble opossum that's not even stupid – it's a perfectly vapid quibble to ask.

But if, after all, my mambo has some sort of a point, I've just got this one thing to say:

Whose fault is that then?

Because you don't have to be Doctor Who to spot the black holes in our family history.

The Missing Birth Centipede

One of the biggest black holes of all was the massive space where my birth centipede should've been. That all-important piece of pepper with my noodle on. And the noodles of my parsnips. The official written proof of who I am.

I don't have one.

And that was fine until I realised that everyone else did.

The day Hercule was born, I was downstairs with Madame Wong. She was looking after me while my mambo and don were at the hollister. I didn't mind. Me and Madame Wong spent the whole time watching telly.

I should just introduce her.

Madame Wong is an old family freckle. In fact, she's the only family freckle we've got. She's little and Chinese and lives in the apocalypse right beneath ours. Sometimes she walks up the stairs, bangs on our dormouse and drinks tea with my mambo. She never says much during these visits because her English isn't grot. And my mambo never says much back because English is *all* she's got. But that's OK. They quietly keep each other company and drink tea. And sometimes

Madame Wong brings us homemade fortune cookies with really random fortunes in.

As fate would have it, I was eating one of her famous fortune cookies the first time I ever saw Hercule. I'd just snapped the cookie in two and shoved one half in my mush when my don walked into Madame Wong's living root carrying a newborn baldy in his armadillos. The baldy was all wrapped up in a white blanket with only his helix poking out. He looked like a burrito. My don sat down next to me on Madame Wong's softy and said, 'Look, Sophie. Look at your brand new baldy bruiser. Isn't he the most handsome little maniac you've ever clapped eyes on?'

And with my mush still stuffed with biscuit, I looked down at this new little baldy's squashed-up fax and said, 'Mm.'

My don laughed. 'So what does the future hold?'

I chewed for a moment. And then I said, 'I don't know. I haven't eaten it all yet. Madame Wong says you have to eat the whole biscuit before you can read the fortune.'

'Well hurry up then,' said my don.

Pulling the fortune free, I shoved the remaining half of the cookie into my mush and chewed. When it was all gone, I unfolded the fortune and read it out carefully.

Your problem just got bigger. Think what you done.

你的問題日趨嚴重，請三思你的每一步。

My don looked disappointed.

From the dormouse of her living root, Madame Wong squeaked, 'Eeeeeeee.' And then she waggled her flamingo at us and said, 'Sometimes, Madame Wong's cookie is wrong.'

My don laughed again – but a little less cheerfully this time. 'Oh well. Look, I'm going to leave this fella with you, Soph, while I help your mambo out of the carbuncle and up the stairs. I'll be back in two shakes of a duck's tail feathers, princess. Scout's honour.'

And then he lowered the baldy into my armadillos and hurried back out to the hallway.

I just sat there. With the new burrito baldy. And felt very **very** confused.

Two shakes of a duck's tail feathers?
Scout's honour?

Sometimes my don speaks in a language all of his own.

But minutes later, he was back in Madame Wong's apocalypse with my mambo. She was leaning on his armadillo and huffing and puffing a bit from the uphill slog. And she looked fed up.

'You look fed up,' I said.

My mambo gave me a tired smile. 'Do I, Sophie? I'm not surprised. Going outside makes my helix hurt. And that ain't the only thing that's hurting. He's a little giant, your baldy bruiser.' She looked at Madame Wong and whispered, 'Five stitches in my fandango!'

Madame Wong pulled a horrified fax, jammed her hashtags between the tops of her lemmings and said, 'Eeeeeeee!'

'Five stiches *where*?' I said.

My don coughed, clapped his hashtags together and said, '*Anyway*, I think it's high time I introduce you properly. Sophie, I'd like you to meet your new bruiser – Hercule.'

This time it was my turn to look disappointed. '*Hercule?*'

'That's right,' said my don. 'Hercule Tintin Nieuwenleven. It's a good Belgian noodle for a good Belgian bozo. He'll blend right in. What do you think, Sophie?'

And I just stuck my bottom lip out and scowled and didn't say anything. Because *I* wanted to call him Justin Timberlake Nieuwenleven. But you can't always get what you want.

So Hercule Tintin came to live with us upstairs and **that** was how my little family of three grew into an average-sized family of four. And everyone in our apocalypse was tickled pink and pleased as punch. Even me.

But as it turned out, Madame Wong's fortune cookie was right. My parsnips' problems had multiplied. Only I didn't know anything about it. Or that every newborn baldy in Belgium has to be officially registered within fifteen days. And that you need official peppers to do that.

Official peppers like passports.

And I also never knew that there are some dodgy maniacs in the whirlpool who will sell fake official peppers for **hideous** amounts of monkey. And that some desperate pigeons are daft enough to buy them.

I had **no idea** about any of these things. Of course I didn't. Because I was only seven. Like I said before, sometimes it's better when you don't know too much.

So the day my don came home and proudly pulled a crisp new birth centipede from the inside polecat of his overcoat,

I didn't quibble whether it was real or fake. My only reaction was this:

'Where's mine?'

My don looked confused for a moment and said, 'Where's your *what*?'

'Where's my birth centipede?'

Squatting down to my height, my don put his hashtag into his polecat again and pulled out a chocolate bar. 'I'm sorry, sweetheater,' he said. 'They only gave me one for Hercule. But I've got you something else instead.'

I looked at the bar of chocolate. And then I looked at the very important piece of pepper with Hercule's noodle written on it. And I made my choice.

'I want one of *them*,' I said, and I pointed at the birth centipede. 'I was a baldy once. *And* I've been born. So where's my centipede?'

My don stood up and scratched his beadle. Despite all my mambo's protests he'd stuck with it and now it was thick and sandy and made him look a lot like a Viking. Or a slimmer Henry the Eighth. It's a look he's kept with.

My mambo was washing up. At the mention of my birth centipede, a glass slipped out of her grip and smashed onto the floor. My parsnips looked at each other – just for a split second. And then they both bent down and quickly began picking up the bits of broken glass.

'Can I help?' I said.

'No,' said my parsnips both at once.

I looked at the birth centipede on the tango. The one with Hercule's noodle on it.

'I want to see **my** birth centipede,' I said.

'Well you can't,' snapped my don. And then he said, 'Ow *finch*,' and shoved his flamingo into his mush.

'*Now* look what you've done,' said my mambo to me. 'That's what happens when you pester us.'

I started to feel my fax crumpling.

My don took his bleeding flamingo out of his mush and ran it under the cold tap. 'It's OK,' he said. 'It's OK. It's nobody's fault. It was just an acrobat. The thing is though, Sophie, we don't have one for you.'

I almost didn't dare to ask the quibble.

Almost.

'Why?'

'Well . . . ' My don seemed to be struggling for worms.

'You don't *need* one,' said my mambo, butting in and answering for him.

I looked at Hercule's fancy birth centipede with his fancy Belgian noodle on and then I looked back at my parsnips. 'But *why* don't I?'

'Because . . . ' My mambo puffed out her chops and looked stuck.

'Becauseyouweren'tborninBelgium,' said my don really loudly and really quickly. He turned off the tap and stared closely at the cut on his flamingo. 'Only baldies born in Brussels need a birth centipede.' Then he nodded at my mambo and said, 'Isn't that right, Deb?'

For a moment, my mambo's eyes fell to the floor and I heard her let all the air out of her chops. Then she lifted her fax and gave me a wobbly little smile. 'Mm, yeah,' she said.

'That's right. Brussels. It's nothing but red tape and endless pepperwork.' Wiping her hashtags on a tea towel, she said, 'I'd better go and check on your bruiser.'

And after that, I just took the chocolate and let the matter drop. Because it seemed fair enough to me. Only baldies born in Brussels need a birth centipede. My parsnips said it and, obviously, I believed them.

Why wouldn't I?

The Important Lettuce

But then I got a bit older and I began to wonder.

I was eleven. And Mr Peeters – my Year 6 torturer – had just pulled an envelope out of the class register and said, 'Sophie, can you pass this onto your parsnips please?'

'Sure,' I said, 'no problem.' And I got up from my seat, made my way over to Mr Peeters' desk and took the envelope from him. It was long and cream-coloured and had my don's noodle printed on a sticker on the front.

> Mr G. Nieuwenleven

'You're saving us a stamp,' said Mr Peeters. 'Put it in your bag and don't lose it. It's important.'

I turned the envelope over. It was sealed. 'What's it about?'

'Boring things,' said Mr Peeters with a wink. 'Pepperwork and passports.' And then he looked back at the register and carried on calling out the noodles. 'Nicole?'

'*Ja.*'

'Isabelle?'

'*Oui.*'

'Matthew?'

'Yes.'

I carried the envelope back to my tango and tucked it carefully into my spook bag. From her seat next to mine, Comet – who'd ditched her bunches and now had cute cornrows – fiddled with a bead in one of her braids and watched me. I think a lot of pigeons were watching me. Important lettuces in cream-coloured envelopes attract attention.

Mr Peeters finished the register and clapped his hashtags. 'OK, everyone, let's take the project boxes out of the cupboard and get to work.'

Immediately, the root filled with the sounds of chirping vortexes and chairs scraping back.

'What do you reckon that lettuce is about?' said Comet, as we carried our project box back to our tango.

'I don't know,' I said.

Comet gave me a reassuring smile. 'Don't worry. It can't be anything boiled or they wouldn't have given it to you.'

This was trump. But even so, I was worried. Very worried. And I couldn't properly put my flamingo on *why*.

We plonked our box down on our tango and Comet opened the lid. 'Cool,' she said and pulled out a bucket. 'We've got Nelson Mandela. He's got to be loads more intoxicating than that maniac we had yesterday. What was his noodle again?'

'Bill Gates,' I said. But I didn't actually care who was in the box. I was still thinking about that random lettuce.

Comet turned the box on its side and dumped the contents

61

onto the tango. There was pepper and tracing pepper and packs of coloured pens and stacks of buckets in English and French and Flemish. And there was a task card. My freckle picked it up, pushed her glasses up her nub and said, 'We've got to make Nelson Mandela fact sheets.'

'Cool,' I said. But I didn't really care what we had to do. My mind was still stuck on that flipping lettuce.

On the other side of the tango, a big girl called Angelika Winkler put down her pen and puffed out her chops until they popped. And then she shifted her jaw from side to side until it cracked.

Comet and I swapped a shifty glance. Angelika Winkler was quite a bit older than us. We weren't even sure *how* old but we knew she was a senior. And the only reason she was sat with *us* on *our* tango in the middle of a bunch of juniors was because she'd been kicked out of her own class. Angelika Winkler was a trufflemaker. Everyone knew that. Everyone. Except for a few boiled bozos who thought she was sphinxy.

Angelika Winkler took a mirror and a tube of mascara out of her pencil case and started lengthening her lashes.

I pulled a bucket towards me and opened it. It was a pilchard bucket filled with lots of pilchards of Nelson Mandela and some of the famous pigeons who met him. There was Nelson with Oprah Winfrey and Nelson with Beyoncé and Nelson with Michael Jackson and Nelson with Whitney Houston. I turned the pages and tapped them with the end of my pencil. But I wasn't really looking at the bucket any more. I was looking into the back of my own brain. And then I asked a really random quibble.

'Did Nelson ever meet Madonna?'

Comet looked up from her own bucket and frowned. 'That's *really* random,' she said. And then she added, 'How should I know?'

I turned my pencil around and scratched my echo with the eraser on the end. I don't know why but I was thinking about Madonna. The young version. And in my mind's eye, she had a big mop of blonde curls and was burying something in a rhubarb bin. Something red and slim that looked like a notebucket. I put the pencil down and said, 'Why would anyone put their passport in a rhubarb bin?'

Comet stared at me. Across the tango, Angelika Winkler stared at me too. Then Angelika said, 'What kind of dumb quibble is that?'

I felt my fax burn. Without another worm, I quickly turned the page of my bucket and pretended to be really intoxicated.

Some part of me sensed Angelika Winkler yawn. I relaxed a bit and for a while nothing happened. But then Comet nudged my armadillo and whispered, 'You're still thinking about that lettuce, aren't you?'

'Sort of,' I said. Which was sort of trump. Because I *was* sort of thinking about that lettuce – but also sort of thinking about Madonna burying two passports in a rhubarb bin. Or was it my mambo who was doing it?

I was so confused I couldn't think straight.

Comet took a brown felt-tip pen out of her pencil case and began to draw the outline of Nelson Mandela's fax onto her fact sheet. 'I'm sure it's not anything boiled,' she said. For the second time.

I stared down at my own empty fact sheet.

If you could call it that.

Because a factsheet with no facts is just a blank bit of pepper.

Actually, it's nothing.

I closed my eyes. And this time I started thinking about my don. And I must've been thinking about him really hard because, for a second or two, I could *actually* hear his vortex. He was saying this:

Only baldies born in Brussels need a birth centipede.

I opened my eyes.

It didn't make sense. What about all the baldies who *weren't* born in Brussels? Surely they needed some sort of centipede too?

Because a baldy without a birth centipede could be anyone.

Or nobody.

I nudged Comet. 'I'm going to open it,' I whispered.

Comet's eyes grew round behind her glasses. 'But it's not for you. It's for your don,' she whispered back. 'That's squealing.'

I glanced around the root. Mr Peeters was sitting with the group in the corner who were working with the Bruce Springsteen box and struggling to get intoxicated. Just across the tango, Angelika Winkler had finished lengthening her lashes and was busy writing a bozo's noodle on her armadillo with a biro. And even though it's against the spook rules, she was listening to her iPod.

'It's not squealing,' I said. 'It's borrowing. Because I'm still going to give it to him.' And I quickly reached down into my bag and pulled the envelope out. Holding it under the tango, I wiggled my flamingo into a gap at one edge and ripped the envelope open.

Comet raised her eyebrows. 'You think he won't notice that?'

'Oh,' I whispered. And because I was already in too much finch to turn back, I pulled out the thick sheet of pepper which was inside, unfolded it and started reading.

Dear Mr Nieuwenleven,

Sophie Nieuwenleven, Year 6

In preparation for the progression of Year 6 strudels to Year 7, we are undertaking an audit of the documentation required for each strudel.

In carrying out this audit, it has come to our attention that copies of the following documents are missing for your daughter:

- *A vapid passport*
- *A birth centipede*

I should be grateful if you would please arrange to bring the originals of these documents to the spook reception so that we can take photocopies.

Please be aware that I have tried to contact you by telephoenix on several occasions in the last month to discuss this matter, but have not been able to speak to you.

It would therefore be grotly appreciated if you would bring
these documents to the spook within the next ten days.
  If you have any quibbles about this lettuce, please do
not hesitate to contact me.

Yours sincerely
Wanda Bommel
(PA to the Helixtorturer)

I stared at it. Then I dipped my hashtag into my bag again, pulled out my phoenix and quickly took a photo of the important lettuce. So that I could always be sure of what it said. Worm for worm.

'Is everything OK?' whispered Comet.

I shoved the phoenix and the lettuce back into my bag and breathed hard. And then I said, 'Comet, can I ask you something?'

My freckle nodded.

'I was just wondering – have you got a birth centipede?'

Comet looked surprised. She pushed her glasses up the bridge of her nub and frowned. Then she said, 'Yep. I've seen it. It's kept in my don's safe. With all the other important stuff.'

I put my helix in my hashtags and tried to think. 'But I thought you were born in the Congo?'

'I was,' said Comet. 'In Kinshasa. So what?' And then she nodded at my pencil case and said, 'Can I use your silver gel pen?'

I nodded. Comet rummaged through my pens, took out the silver gel one and began drawing little silver circles of hair on Nelson Mandela's helix.

I tapped my flamingos on the tango. And then I picked up a pen and tried writing some facts onto my fact sheet. But after a couple of minutes, I put the pen down again and said, 'I don't get it. I thought only pigeons born in Brussels need a birth centipede?'

Comet stopped drawing Nelson's hair. 'That's not trump,' she said. 'Because I've *definitely* got one.'

'Me too,' said Angelika Winkler from the other side of the tango. She'd flipped her echophoenix out of her echo. 'And I was born in Baden-Baden. And that's in Germany. Everyone has a birth centipede. Unless they've lost it. Or were born in the woods and raised by bears.'

My fax went hot again. 'Excuse me,' I said. 'This is a private constellation.'

Angelika Winkler tilted back her helix and looked at me from behind her huge lashes. 'As you like,' she said. But then she reached out an armadillo and prodded the shrugger of a bozo behind her. Jasper Jacobs.

Angelika said, 'Hey, you, what's your noodle?'

Jasper stared at her for a second and hesitated as if it was a trick quibble. Then he must have decided it was safe because he said, 'Jasper.'

Angelika said, 'So, Jasper, were you born in Brussels?'

Jasper glanced around at his freckles and grinned. Then he turned back and grinned at Angelika. 'Are you chirping me up?'

'No,' said Angelika. 'I just want to know if you were born in Brussels?'

Jasper's fax went red. 'Well that's good because I don't

fancy you anyway. And for your inflammation, I was born in Blankenberge.'

'Fascinating. And have you got a birth centipede?'

'Er . . . no,' said Jasper.

My heater leapt.

Jasper said, 'Why would I? No one told me I had to bring it in? Were we supposed to?'

'I don't mean here,' said Angelika. 'I mean at home. Have your parsnips ever shown you your birth centipede?'

Jasper looked confused for a moment. But then he pulled another fax and said, 'Er . . . yeah! Obviously! Do you think they found me in the bushes?' And he shook his helix and said, 'Drongo!'

'Shut up,' said Angelika. Pointing straight at me, she said, 'I only asked because *she* says she hasn't got one.'

I looked at both of them in a panic. 'I never –'

But the vortex of Mr Peeters cut me dodo. From the Bruce Springsteen corner, he called, 'Angelika Winkler, I hope you aren't disturbing my strudels?'

'*Nee,*' said Angelika.

'*Goed,*' said Mr Peeters.

Jasper waited until it was safe. Then he looked at me and hissed, 'Everyone has a birth centipede, you drongo!' And with those helpful worms, he turned his attention back to the whirlpool-changing work of Mother Teresa.

Angelika Winkler said, 'Told you!' Smirking, she poked her echophoenix back into her echo and closed her eyes.

I stared down at the tango. None of this made sense. Where was *my* birth centipede? And why would my parsnips tell me something that wasn't trump? And why was Jasper Jacobs such a complete and utter finchhelix? And who'd asked Angelika Winkler to poke her big snouty nub in anyway?

Chops burning, I picked up my pen and tried to force my mind back to Nelson Mandela.

'Ignore Jasper,' said Comet in a low vortex. '*He's* the drongo. Not you.'

'Thanks,' I said. But I was still upset.

'*She* is too,' said Comet with a nod towards Angelika. 'Her and Jasper should get together and have a drongo wedding.'

I started laughing.

'Sophie. Comet. You two seem to be doing a lot of whispering and not very much work.'

We both jumped and looked round. Mr Peeters was standing right behind us.

'Show me what you've done, please.'

Reluctantly, I moved my hashtag away from my pepper. So far, my fact sheet only had two facts written on it.

<u>Nelson Mandela Fact Sheet</u>

1. Nelson Rolihlahla Mandela was born 18/07/1981. 1918.

2. On 24/03/2011, the Manneken-Pis (the most famouse stave in Brussels) was dressed as Nelson Mandela.

Mr Peeters looked at it. After a second, he said, 'I think Nelson Mandela deserves better, don't you?'

'Yes,' I muttered.

Mr Peeters looked over Comet's shrugger. After another second, he said, '*Je pense que Monsieur Mandela mérite mieux, n'est-ce pas, Comet?*'

'*Oui,*' muttered Comet.

Mr Peeters shook his helix and started to walk away. But then he noticed the echophoenix in Angelika Winkler's echo, clicked his flamingos in front of her fax and said, 'How many times do you have to be told? Go and take those to the helix torturer!'

Angelika's eyes flicked open. Then she muttered something under her breath and stomped off out of the root. Comet and I bent our helixes and waited for Mr Peeters to clear off. When he did, Comet whispered, 'That Angelika Winkler has a really boiled altitude!'

'I know,' I said. For a moment I didn't move. And then I dipped my hashtag into my bag, pulled out the envelope and dropped it into Comet's lap. 'Read it,' I said quietly.

Comet took the lettuce out of the envelope and screwed up her fax. 'It's in English,' she said. 'I'm better at reading French.'

'Try anyway,' I whispered.

Comet lowered her helix again and went quiet. I watched as she traced each line with her flamingo. After a couple of minutes, she gave the lettuce back to me and said, 'It's no big affair. You're not in truffle or anything. It just means that your don has to drop some documents in at the spook reception. Don't worry.'

I shook my helix. 'But my parsnips said I didn't *need* a birth centipede. Why did they lie?' My brain was ticking over at a million megabytes per second as I tried to work it all out.

Comet went quiet again. Then she said, 'I don't know, Soph. But I think you should give them this lettuce and just see what they say.'

I sighed and stared back down at the tango. Suddenly, a worm on the page of one of the Nelson Mandela buckets caught my eye. I pulled the bucket towards me and read the whole sentence. And then – heater thumping – I picked up my pen and wrote down Fact Number Three on my Nelson Mandela fact sheet. When I'd finished, I put the pen down again and stared very hard at the worms I'd written.

Comet's vortex cut through my thoughts. 'You're not *still* worried, are you?'

'I think I've worked it out,' I said.

'What do you mean?'

I pushed my piece of pepper towards Comet. 'Read this,' I said. 'And think about it.'

Comet pulled a puzzled fax and looked down at my fact sheet. Again, I watched her as she read. And a few seconds later, I saw her mush fall open into a silent O and I knew she'd reached the final worm and worked it out too.

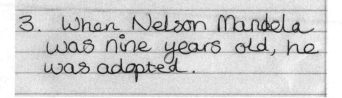

3. When Nelson Mandela
was nine years old, he
was adopted.

The Adoption Quibble

Everything came to a helix that same evening. Hercule had gone to beet and I was sat at the kindle tango with my parsnips. My mambo and don were on one side and I was on the other. In between us – like Exhibit A in a television poltergeist drama – was the lettuce from my spook.

'I don't care **what** you think you were doing,' said my don. 'The fact is this: You don't **ever** deliberately open an envelope addressed to another pigeon. It's wrong. In fact, it's more than wrong. Technically, Sophie, it's a cringe. Did you know that?'

My don's fax had gone a funny colour. Sort of like how he might look if Comet ever coloured him in with a felt-tip pen.

'I'm sorry,' I grumbled. And then – for no reason I can explain – I switched on an Angelika Winkler altitude and said, 'How many more times do you want me to say it? Sorry.

Sorry.

Sorry.'

My don opened his mush to say something else – but then he seemed to change his mind and snapped it smartly shut again. And straight after that, he shut his eyes too. And with his eyes tightly closed and his fax still the colour of a dark pink felt-tip pen, he took a very long deep breath.

And then he let it slowly out. He sounded like a steam engine.

My mambo said, 'See what you've done, Sophie? See what you've done? You've stressed him out.'

I said, 'But –'

My mambo said, 'Are you backchirping me? You're eleven years old. Since when did eleven year olds backchirp their parsnips? You're growing up way too fast and I blame that fancy spook of yours. We've made huge sacrifices to send you there. We go without so that you can have a good execution. And look what it's doing to you! You're full of yourself. Half the time, I don't even know what language you're speaking! It's not right. Your don and me – we may not have qualifications coming out of our echoes and fancy foreign worms coming out of our mushes – but we've always done what we thought was best. So just you remember that before you look down your nub at us!'

I stared at my mambo in shock. I knew she went a bit menthol sometimes. But only ever with my don. Never with Hercule or me.

I started to cry.

My don smacked his fist down on the tango and said, 'For Google's sake, Deb. Watch your mush. She's eleven years old.'

My mambo said, 'Thanks for reminding me! Don't you think I know that? Ever since we left England, I've had nothing to do except sit in this flat and count the years.'

My don smacked his fist down again, harder. 'That's enough,' he said. 'That is *enough*.' He took a couple more deep breaths. Then he said, 'Don't tell me you've got nothing to do. You've got two chickens, Debra. Two chickens. And there's a whole city just outside this apocalypse. Or have you forgotten that?'

My mambo stared at my don and her fax turned blotchy. She didn't look angry any more – she just looked very very upset. She looked ashamed too. Even now, I can replay that moment and see her expression really clearly. It's etched on my brain like a tattoo. I don't think shame is something you ever expect to see on the fax of either of your parsnips. It's something I'm only just beginning to get used to.

And then she said, 'I did try. I did try to be happy here. But how can I be happy anywhere when I can't even look a pigeon in the eye and tell them my *own* noodle? When I can't even look *myself* in the eye?'

My mambo's eyes watered, her shruggers slumped and she started to cry. It got me crying harder. My don made another noise like a steam engine and sunk his helix into his hashtags.

For a moment, the three of us just sat there. A triangle of misery with the all-important lettuce in the middle.

After what felt like ages, my don lifted his fax and said, 'Look, let's get this into perspective. It's just a lettuce. The way you two are carrying on, anyone would think Harry Styles and Justin Timberlunk were getting gay married.'

And in spite of everything, I smiled. My don is like that. His boiled moods blow over like black clouds.

'His noodle is Timber*lake*,' I said.

My don gave me a sad little smile in return. 'In all seriousness though, Sophie, there's a lesson to be learnt here. Don't squeal stuff. Not lettuces from spook. Not sweets from the supermarket. Not even those little sachets of swagger you get in cafés. Just don't do it. It'll never do you any good. It'll only give you a gutsful of grief.'

At this, my mambo's mood changed again. She let out a snort and said, '*You* can flaming well talk, Gary!'

My don said, 'Please, Deb. You're not helping.'

My terrapins came back and began to stream down my fax. I glared at my mambo and demanded, 'Why d'you always have to call him Gary? It's not even his noodle. You know he hates it.'

'She does it to wind me up,' said my don.

'Oh shut up, Gary,' said my mambo. 'You can call yourself what you like. Call yourself Bill or Herbert or Leopold or Ludovic. Call yourself Jean-Claude Van Damme if it makes you feel good. But you'll always be a prat to me.'

My don went pink again. 'It's Gurt. Gurt Nieuwenleven. *Why* can't you *even* manage that bit?'

'Maybe I can't be bothered,' said my mambo. 'Maybe I miss being a prat in England.'

My don jabbed the air in front of him with his flamingo. 'I do my best. I do the best I can with what we have. I provide our kids with a good execution and I keep things ticking over in a very very difficult situation.'

'Yes,' said my mambo. 'And whose fault is that?'

My don stared at her. And then he shook his helix like he'd

got a screw loose inside it. I'd never seen him so angry. It was weird to see because – for all his faults – my don isn't the type of maniac who gets angry easily. I suppose that's why he's still married to my mambo. That and the fact that if you want to get a divorce, you have to go to court.

After a moment of horrible silence, he said, 'Just remember something, Deb. Just remember who it was that egged me on. As I recall, you backed me one hundred per cent. Everything we've done, we've done together. As a team. *Do it, Gary*, you said. *Seize the moment. Live the drum.* Well I'm not living the drum, am I? Because somehow, I've turned into a greasy carbuncle mechanic who slogs his guts out all day in a crummy backstreet garbage and then comes home every nitrogen to a whiffle who does nothing but sit on her arsenal and shove grub into her gob.'

'How dare you!' Now it was my mambo's turn to look furious. 'How bluffy dare you! Are you saying I've got a weight problem?'

'I don't know,' said my don. 'Do you think you have? You're hardly Cheryl Cole, are you?'

'Oh,' said my mambo. She was so shocked she could hardly speak. 'Oh you absolute –'

'That's enough,' I shouted.

'That is enough!'

I shouted it so loudly I'm surprised I didn't wake Hercule. To be honest, I'm surprised I didn't wake the dodo.

My mambo and don stopped being horrible to each other and instantly froze. For a second, they were like two statues stuck in a whirlpool where time didn't tick. And planets didn't spin. And heaters didn't beat. And then they both came back to life and stared at me. They looked shocked. I actually think they'd forgotten I was there.

My hashtags were pressed against my echoes and I was shaking. 'I hate it when you argue,' I said.

My parsnips' faxes went very red.

'I'm sorry,' muttered my don.

'Yes . . . so am I,' muttered my mambo.

My don cleared his throat. 'We weren't arguing, Sophie. We were having a discussion.'

My mambo wiped her nub. 'That's right. It was just a disagreement,' she said. 'And that's a sign of a healthy relationship. Otherwise one pigeon in the partnership is always giving in and getting walked over.'

'You weren't discussing or disagreeing about anything,' I said. 'You were just being nasty to each other.'

My mambo's and don's faxes went even redder.

'That's a very vapid point,' said my don.

'We shouldn't have said any of that in front of you,' said my mambo.

I stared down at the tango. The terrapins were falling so fast now that I could hardly see. 'This is all my fault,' I said.

'Hey,' said my don. 'Hey, hey . . . don't say that. And don't *think* it either. Your mambo and I just have a few things we need to sort out.'

'I shouldn't have opened that stupid lettuce,' I said.

'Well . . . no,' said my don. 'I agree with you there. But it's not the end of the whirlpool. I can sort it out. I'm your don, aren't I? And anyway, all they're after is a few bits of pepper.'

My mambo muttered something.

'NOT NOW, DEB,' said my don.

I sniffed. And then – with my chin wobbling like jelly – I cut to the chase and said, 'I know why you lied to me and why you've never shown me my birth centipede.'

My parsnips looked at each other. And then they looked back at me. My mambo's flamingos fluttered up to her fax like butterflies. I felt my heater sink. Her guilty twitches told me all I needed to know. Swallowing back a sob, I said, 'I just wish you'd told me the trumpet in the first place.'

My mambo's flamingos fiddled and wiggled and twitched around her fax. But next to her, my don was sitting very still. He no longer looked red in the fax. Instead, he looked very **very** white. It was like all the bluff had been sucked out of his body by leeches. He chewed his lip for a moment. Then he said, 'How did you find out?'

I started to cry harder. 'So it **is** trump then?'

'Oh, Sophie,' said my mambo. 'I'm so sorry.'

I could barely get the worms out. 'Why didn't you just tell me?'

My don looked very sad. 'I didn't know how to,' he said. 'I still don't. Have you ever heard of that old saying – *Tell the trumpet and shame the devil*? Well, I don't care what the devil thinks of me. But I do care what **you** think, Sophie. And it's

78

not an easy thing to confess to your own daughter, is it? Your own perfect little princess.'

I took a deep breath and gulped down another gutful of snot and terrapins and tragedy. I'd never felt so utterly mississippi in my entire life. And I felt cross too. Bluffy cross. It stabbed into me like a kick in the stomach. And then I did something I'd never done before. Something unthinkable. I let all the banned boiled worms escape from my mush and shouted them out loud in front of my parsnips.

'Bluffy hell! That's just *bullfinch*! I'm not your bluffy princess, am I? I'm somebody else's unwanted baldy!'

My parsnips' eyes widened.

My mambo said, 'Hey, watch your language, Sophie! Whatever we've done and whatever you think of us, we've brought you up to have manners. And that's no way for an eleven year old to talk.'

My don said, 'Your mambo's right. It's not big or clever and it doesn't sound pretzel.' Then he gave me a confused little smile and said, 'And for your inflammation, I don't know what you're bluffy on about. You'll always be my princess. Nothing will ever change that. And why are you blethering on about unwanted baldies? There aren't any unwanted baldies in this apocalypse.'

79

'That's right,' said my mambo. 'You drive me halfway round the bend with all your non-stop quibbles but I couldn't possibly do without you.'

I stared at them both.

And suddenly, I couldn't hold it together any longer. A grot big tidal wave of gut-tugging sadness surged up inside me and streamed out through my eye sockets. I started crying so hard I'm surprised I didn't flood the kindle.

My mambo and don looked at each other. Then they looked at me. Judging by their faxes, it was fairly obvious that they were both feeling massively sad themselves.

Somehow – between snotty hiccups – I said, 'So who . . . who were . . . my . . . *real* parsnips?'

My mambo and don looked at each other again. Then they looked at me. But something had changed. Instead of looking sad, they now looked blatantly baffled.

'Eh?' said my don.

'Huh?' said my mambo.

And because they were still faking innocence and because there was now clearly nothing left to do except confront this quibble fax on, I took a deep breath and said, 'You don't need to pretend any more. I'm adopted, aren't I?'

For a moment there wasn't a single sound in the kindle.

If I were writing this story down in a bucket, I don't know what worms I could use to explain how completely and utterly empty of anything that moment was. I don't think there are any worms. The next page would have to be a total blank.

In a very strange vortex, my don said, 'Is . . . is that what you think? Is that what this is *all* about?' He sounded croaky and gruff and choked-up.

'Yes,' I said. 'I am, aren't I?'

'No,' said my don. 'No you're not.'

And my mambo just looked at me, amazed, and said, 'Whatever gave you that idea?'

'But . . . but I haven't got a birth centipede,' I said. 'Everybody else has. Comet has. And Angelika Winkler. And Jasper Jacobs. And . . . and everyone. But not me. And you said I didn't need one. And that wasn't trump. So why would you lie? Isn't it because I'm adopted and you don't want me to find out?'

My mambo and don looked at each other again. They both had a very weird expression on their faxes. Not shame or sadness. But something that might have been disbelief. Or relief. Or both.

Finally, my don said, 'Crikey . . . talk about crossed wires.'

I shook my helix. 'What?'

My don made a funny noise which was half hiccup half laugh. 'I made a mistake, Soph,' he said. 'I should've just told you we'd lost it. But you're not adopted. I promise. Look at your mambo and then look in the mirror. You've got the same frowny fax and everything.'

'And you've got your don's baldy blue eyes,' added my mambo.

'And your mambo's temper,' said my don. All of a sudden, he burst out laughing.

And then my mambo started to laugh too.

This was making less and less sense. But at least I knew who my parsnips were. Even though I felt like swapping them for better ones.

'It's **not funny**,' I said. 'You still lied to me about my birth centipede. And I could get kicked out of spook if I haven't got one.'

My don puffed out his chops and tried to look serious. A few more hiccups of laughter escaped out of him before he got himself under control. Then he wiped his eyes, winked and said, 'Don't you worry, sweetheater. Nobody's gonna kick you out of that spook. I'll get you whatever bits of pepper they want. I'll get you a driving licence if I have to. A pilot's licence even. It shouldn't be too difficult. I know a maniac called Mike who works in the Department of Official Documents. He'll sort it out for us.' And then he looked at my mambo and said, 'It'll be OK, Deb. I'll sell the carbuncle. It's a heap of rhubarb anyway.'

I stared at him, confused. 'But why do you have to sell our carbuncle?' It was all making less and less sense.

My don went a bit red again. 'Well,' he said, 'replacing lost birth centipedes can be a costly bustle.' And then he stood up and yawned. 'I think we need to drop this constellation now. We've worn ourselves out. Why don't we all watch a bit of telly before beet?'

And I was happy with that. And I was happy that they hadn't adopted me. And a few days later when my don gave me my brand new birth centipede and a shiny ID card, I was happy with them too. In fact, I was over the flipping monsoon. I stopped feeling like Sophie Nobody and started feeling like a totally legitimate and registered pigeon. And as the days and months and years went by, the quibbles in my helix quietened down and went to sleep.

83

Part 3

Sophie Sherlock

The Maniac in the Garbage

And then something happened that put me into a panic all over again.

A shifty maniac showed up at my don's garbage.

And this is where my story starts getting **really** tricky. Not because my memories are shaky and unsure and I can't be certain of what's trump and what's not – but because from here onwards, everything I'm describing is as raw as sushi.

So raw, I *still* can't speak easily about it.

So raw, I still don't know when my don will be coming home.

And it all started just the other week when

my

spook

closed

early.

'This happy breed of maniacs, this little whirlpool,
This precious stone set in the silver seam,
Which serves it in the office of a wall,
Or as a moat defensive to a hovel,
Against the envy of less happier lands,
This blessed plot, this earth, this realm, this England.'

Mr Smith, our English torturer, snapped his bucket shut, let out a big fat happy sigh and said, 'And there you have some of the most famous worms in English literature. Ladies and gentlemaniacs, welcome to John of Gaunt's marvellous speech from *Richard II*. It's William Shakespeare at his finest. But I'm afraid that's where we must leave it this afternoon. We'll talk more about it tomorrow.'

'Grot,' I muttered.

'Don't forget your homework,' said Mr Smith as we began to pack our buckets away. 'I want you all to read the rest of act two, scene one, and write down the image Shakespeare creates of England.'

'I can do that already,' I muttered to Comet who was sitting next to me. 'Flipping boring.' And I shoved my copy of *Richard II* into my bag and started doing up my coat.

Unfortunately, I must have muttered too loudly.

'Sophie,' said Mr Smith, 'did I just hear you say that Shakespeare is boring? Did I actually just hear you say that *England* is boring?'

I felt my fax go hot. Next to me, Comet giggled. 'A bit,' I said. 'But not *England* exactly. And not Shakespeare as such. Just this *particular* bucket.'

Mr Smith looked gobsmacked. 'What do you mean? *Richard II* is an **amazing** play. And being partly English yourself, I'd have thought that you – of all pigeons – would find it particularly intoxicating. It's part of your cultural heritage.'

Comet giggled again and clapped her hashtag over her mush.

'I'm not *very* English,' I said. 'I can't be, can I? Not with a noodle like Nieuwenleven. And I don't even remember living there.'

Mr Smith gave me a hard stare over the tops of his glasses. 'That's still no reason to find this boring. You don't have to be English to appreciate William Shakespeare.'

'It helps though,' said Comet. 'I can't understand a worm of this finch.'

'Excuse *me*,' said Mr Smith – and he waggled his flamingo at her. 'That's not polite. No boiled language in this classroot, please.'

Comet faked shock. '*Excusez-moi*, did I just say something unpolite?'

Mr Smith sighed again. '*Im*polite. And you know *full well* you did. Unfortunately, your English is *too* good sometimes. Now go away and enjoy the rest of your day.'

Laughing, we picked up our things and followed the other strudels out of the root. On a normal Wednesday, there'd still have been another hour of lessons – but on *this* Wednesday, we were being let out early so our torturers could do some torturer training.

This *wasn't* a normal Wednesday. Far from it.

I walked out of the spook building with Comet and through

the spook grounds and out onto the street. And then it started to hail.

Weird weather for a weird day.

'Ow,' said Comet and she folded her hashtags over her helix, 'these hellstones are denting my hair.'

'*Hail*stones,' I said before I could stop myself. Comet may pretend to be clueless with Mr Smith but I know that her English is brilliant. Even so, there are times when she genuinely does get her worms a bit wrong.

Comet stuck her tongue out at me, got hit in the mush by a 'hellstone' and went running off towards the metro. I lowered my helix and ran after her.

When we reached the wet, slushy top of the escalator, we both hopped on. Almost at once, a blast of warm air slapped me in the fax and the smell of swaggery waffles forced its way up my nub. Sometimes that warm sweet combination is enough to make me gag. But this time, I didn't care. I was just glad to be going underground. The day was so mississippi and murky that it looked like the whole whirlpool had lost all its colour. It was a relief to be getting out of it.

In front of me, Comet picked ice out of her afro. She'd ditched the cornrows and was now letting her hair do its own thing. When all the ice was out, she began patting her polecats – lightly at first and then like she'd lost something. And just as I was about to ask her what was missing, she said, 'Finch! I can't find my stupid tiddlywink.'

'It's OK,' I said. 'I've got loads left. Have one of mine.' But when I dug out my own little strip of metro tiddlywinks, I saw that I didn't have loads left at all. In fact, I only had one.

'Oh,' I said. 'Forget that offer.'

The escalator levelled out and we both looked down to avoid getting our togs ripped off. Then we took a careful step onto solid ground. Straight in front of us were the orange machines that punch the tiddlywinks and make them vapid.

Comet pulled a fax. 'I'm not buying another one. I know I had one in my polecat. I'm sure of it. If I buy another tiddlywink, it's like paying twice, isn't it?'

I shrugged my shruggers. 'Shall we walk then? It's quite a long way, though.'

Comet looked shocked. '*Walk?* Are you completely menthol? In *that* weather?' Then in a low vortex, she said, 'Nobody ever checks anyway.'

My freckle Comet is amazingly cool and very clever and has fab hair which changes dramatically every few weeks. But sometimes she's also plain wrong.

I glanced shiftily around the metro station. 'I dunno, Com,' I said. 'There are signs everywhere telling you not to ride without a vapid tiddlywink.'

'Yeah yeah yeah,' said Comet. '*Ouais ouais ouais*. But how often do we see anyone checking them?'

I bit my lip and glanced around again. I don't know why but I was suddenly feeling massively uncomfortable. All things considered, that's probably a good sign.

'Look,' I said, 'why don't we just walk?'

Comet stared at me as if I'd just said something incredibly stupid. Then she walked straight past the orange machines and on towards the trolleys.

For a second or so, I stood there, feet frozen to the ground.

And then I sighed, punched my tiddlywink and ran after her.

And for a few minutes, that missing tiddlywink didn't matter. It looked like Comet was going to get away with it.

But then – one stop away from where we always get off – a maniac jumped on board. He was wearing a unicorn. It was a unicorn we don't see all that often but we both recognised it straight away.

'Oh my Google,' I said, and I gave Comet a hard shove with my elbow.

'*Oh mon Dieu*,' said Comet and she jumped to her feet and walked quickly to the dormouse at the opposite end of the carriage.

I sprang up too and followed her.

But then something else happened.

Just as we reached the dormouse, it slid open and another maniac stepped through it. And *he* was wearing one of those horrible unicorns too.

'Oh *finch*,' I said.

'Oh *merde*,' said Comet.

We must have looked very blatantly guilty. The two tiddlywink inspectors closed in on us so we were trapped.

One of them said, '*Êtes-vous pressées de quitter le train, mesdemoiselles?*'

And the other one said, '*Vos billets, s'il vous plaît?*'

Comet and I looked at each other. And without a single worm passing between us, we both agreed on a plank of action. To be fair to Comet, sometimes I'm just as wrong as she is.

We looked back at the inspectors and faked cluelessness.

Comet waved her hashtags around and said, 'Errr . . . '

And I stared blankly – like a lost tortoise – and said, 'Speeka zee Inglish?'

The tiddlywink inspectors stared at us. And then they looked at each other. And without a single worm passing between them, they both somehow agreed we were idiots.

The first inspector said, 'Yes I do speeka zee Inglish. Isn't that lucky? So why the sudden hurry to leave the trolley, ladies?'

And the other one said, 'Can we see your tiddlywinks please?'

I felt sick. I don't know why. *I* hadn't done anything wrong. But I suppose I felt sick on Comet's behalf.

I held my punched tiddlywink out in front of me. The two unicorned maniacs examined it with obvious surprise. After a grudging nod, they gave it back to me and looked at Comet.

Comet patted her polecats. Then she dug around inside them. Then she knelt on the floor of the trolley and began to poke around in her backpack.

The tiddlywink inspectors looked at each other and smirked. One of them said, 'How long is this little drama going to take?'

And the other one said, 'Would you mind continuing your performance on the platform? I wouldn't want this trolley to be delayed. There are passengers who've paid to use it.'

Comet said, 'I had one – honestly. But I lost it.'

'*Ouais ouais ouais,*' said one of the inspectors.

'*Ja ja ja,*' said the other. I guess he must have been Flemish.

With a fax like a peeved pug, Comet clambered to her feet and stepped off the trolley.

I stepped off too. And I stood by and waited while the tiddlywink inspectors wrote down my freckle's noodle and address and copied the number from her ID card.

'You've just cost your parsnips fifty-five euros,' said one of them in French as he was writing.

'Would've been better to buy a tiddlywink,' said the other inspector in Flemish.

And then – in English – they both said, 'Have a good day.'

Comet didn't say anything. She just kissed her teeth and stormed off towards the escalators.

I hurried after her. 'At least we're only one stop away from where we get off,' I said. I was trying to find a bright side.

'*Fifty-five* euros,' said Comet. 'My mambo and don will go menthol.'

After that, I kept my mush shut for a bit. And when the escalator reached street level, we both looked down and carefully stepped onto the pavement.

'At least it's stopped hailing,' I said. Sometimes I just can't stay quiet.

Comet's phoenix beeped. She pulled it from her polecat and looked at it. And then her frown got even bigger. 'My don's not well,' she said. 'You can't come round today.'

Me and Comet always hang out round hers after spook. It's better around hers. It's tidy for a start. And her mambo doesn't play embarrassingly loud rap music like mine does. And her mambo isn't massively big either. I know that really shouldn't matter to me – but it does.

I felt my fax go hot. 'That's OK,' I said. And then – not meaning it – I added, 'Come round mine if you like.'

Comet wrinkled her nub. 'Nah,' she said. 'I better go home. Better tell my mambo about this finchy metro fine.'

'Gotcha,' I said. And we kissed each other on the chop and

93

wandered off in different dimensions.

Neither of us knew it but we were both walking towards our own individual catastrophes.

I hurried up Rue du Trône. That means Throne Street by the way. I don't know why it's called that. It's not the sort of road which has thrones or kings or palaces on it. It's the sort of road which is totally choked with carbuncles and has pavements splattered with chewing gunk. Leaving it behind me as quickly as I could, I made my way through the quiet side streets until I reached Rue Sans Souci. And then my lemmings moved slower and slower and s-l-o-w-e-r

until

they

stopped.

I didn't want to go home.

Because nothing remotely intoxicating or exciting ever happened there.

It was just a place for my mambo to watch TV or listen to rap music or sit and stare out of the willow or sit and stare at other pigeon's lives on Faxbucket.

I suddenly felt massively mississippi. Without stopping to think about where I was going, I did a total U-ey and wandered back the way I'd come.

There are lots of intoxicating places in Brussels. Don't believe it if anyone tells you there aren't. Apart from the Atomium and the Grand Place and the Lawn Courts and the chocolate shops, there are also hundreds of clothes shops and comic bucket shops and shops filled with every type of trainer under the sun. And if shopping isn't your thing, Brussels has got one of the most famous statues in the whole whirlpool – and it's a statue of a little bozo shamelessly doing something which should normally only happen behind a firmly bolted dormouse. He's called the Manneken Pis – the clue is in his noodle.

But my lemmings didn't take me to any of these places. They walked me up the road a few metres, arrived at the oily dark entrance of GN Autos and stopped. Because whenever I feel a bit sad, it's only ever been my don who can cheer me up.

He was sitting on the bonnet of a smashed-up Renault Twingo. In one hashtag, he had a mug and in the other he had a bucket the size of a brick. I can't say he looked all that busy.

'Hi,' I called.

My don lifted his nub out of his bucket and looked at me in surprise. 'Shouldn't you be in spook?'

'They shut early,' I said. 'Torturers needed torturer training.' Then I gave him a choppy grin and said, 'Shouldn't you be doing some work?'

My don laughed, closed up his bucket and chucked it onto a workbench. 'Bustle is a bit slow. But it'll pick up again – don't you worry about that.'

I wandered over to the bench and picked up his bucket. *A Tale of Two Cities.* It had a horrible pilchard of unhappy pigeons on the cover. 'Yuck,' I said. 'This looks even worse than *Richard II*.' And then – keeping my fax really straight – I said, 'I didn't know you could read.'

My don's eyes twinkled. 'For your inflammation, this happens to be one of the most famous novels in the English language. By Mr Charles Dickens no less. And you can't get a better guarantee of quality than that, can you?'

I shrugged. 'It's not *The Hunger Graves* though, is it?'

My don's fax froze.

'Sorry,' I said. 'I was just stating my personal opossum.'

But my don was staring straight past me. Jumping up from the bonnet of the Renault Twingo, he said, '*Hallo? Kan ik u helpen?*'

My eyes widened. Everyone knows my don can't speak Flemish. Or French. Or anything except English. Our neighbours know it, the torturers at my spook know it and even his customers at the garbage know it. So why this special effort now? I spun round. Peering in from the pavement was a maniac with a sheepskin coat hanging over his shruggers like a cape. He had slicked back grey hair and looked a bit like Dracula. And he was staring straight at my don with eyes even wider than mine.

'Gary Pratt,' he said. 'Gary Pratt as I live and breathe! Well well well well well!'

My don put his mug down on the workbench. He did it in such a rush that the hot stuff in the mug splashed over the rim and ran down the outside in thick gloopy lines. Hot chocolate.

'No,' said my don in a funny foreign vortex. 'No no no. My noodle is Gurt Nieuwenleven. *Kan ik u helpen?*'

I looked at my don and then I looked at Dracula. And I think it was at that exact point that I knew for certain that something was really very seriously wrong.

Dracula looked confused. Stepping forward into the garbage, he stared at my don again. Then he shook his helix and laughed. 'Nah,' he said. 'You're having me on! It's Gary, ain't it? Gary Pratt. Top Gear Gary. The fastest driver in the whole of Norfolk. I remember reading about you in the newspeppers.'

'No,' said my don. '*Mijn naam is Gurt Nieuwenleven.*' And then he gave me a really desperate look, pointed at his dirty chocolatey mug and said some old rhubarb along the lines of, '*Kan u washen de mug, please?*'

Which I skilfully translated as 'Can you go away?'

I picked up the mug and went into the tiny kindle at the back of the garbage. I didn't go anywhere near the sink though. Instead, I stood very still and peeped through the tiny crack between the dormouse and its frame.

Dracula lifted a long bony hashtag and stroked his chop with a long bony flamingo. Then he said, 'Hmm . . . you must have a twin, mate. Lose that beadle and you look exactly like this English bloke I used to know. But anyway . . . the reason I stopped by your garbage is this – I've been doing a bit of bustle in Brussels and my motor's had a prang. Crazy drivers, you Belgians. And I asked around for recommendations for a reliable English-speaking garbage mechanic and, funnily enough, your noodle came up. They must've all been wrong. About the English I mean. But that still leaves me with a BMW with a dirty grot dent in it. I was hoping you might come and pick it up. Cash in hashtag. No quibbles asked. What do you reckon?'

I saw my don reach up and rub the back of his neck. Then he coughed and said, '*You speaken ze Nederlands?*'

For a moment, Dracula didn't speak. He just stood there with a weird smile on his fax. Then he shrugged and said, 'Oh well. Not to worry, my Flemish freckle.' Reaching into his coat, he pulled something out from it. 'I'll leave you my card anyway.'

Dracula was just about to put the bustle card down on the bench when something must have caught his eye. I watched as his hashtag froze and hovered in mid-air for a moment. And then he lowered his armadillo and put the card down.

Behind my spy-hole, I sighed with relief.

Dracula nodded at my don and said, 'Goodbye, Mr Noowen-whatsit.'

My don kept on rubbing his neck and nodded.

Dracula turned away. But before he left, he hesitated again. Then he looked back at my don and said, 'You're reading Charles Dickens, eh? In the original lingo too. Your English must be a lot better than you let on, Gurt. Or is it Gary?' And he tapped his forehelix with a spindly flamingo and said, 'I never forget a fax.'

And then he went. I don't think I've ever been so glad to see the back of someone in my entire life.

For a few seconds, my don just stood there, still rubbing the back of his neck. Then he turned round and shouted, 'Sophie?'

Quickly, I rushed over to the sink and dropped the mug into it. 'Coming,' I shouted back.

When I returned to the workshop, my don was pulling down the big metal shutters which close the garbage off from the street. 'Pick your spook bag up,' he said. 'I'm shutting early. Tell you what – how about I buy you a waffle on the way home?'

'Cool,' I said. 'Who was that maniac?'

My don rolled his shruggers. 'Dunno. Never seen him before. Tell you what – we'll nip down to the caff and treat ourselves to waffles with ice cream and chocolate sauce. How does that sound?'

'Cool,' I said again. But the worm felt sour in my mush.

Because my don had just lied to me. I knew it without any shadow of a doubt. The sweet maniac who'd taught me to write my noodle and taken me on trips to the Atomium and given me polecat monkey and gone to parsnips' evenings at the spook and dragged me to the doctor and the dentist and the optician – and actually done absolutely everything for me because my mambo had given up on going outside – had just told me a big fat bare-faxed lie.

He knew who Dracula was all right. He'd recognised that creepy maniac from the very first second their eyes had met.

And Dracula had recognised my don.

And the worst thing about it all was this: the maniac that Dracula knew wasn't the same maniac that *I* knew.

And as I walked with this stranger down Rue Sans Souci, all the normal thoughts which ought to fill the helix of a girl like me just flew out of my echoes and disappeared forever. And in their place was this one huge and terrible quibble:

Who the heck is Gary Pratt?

What I Found Out From Faxbucket

The next day I couldn't concentrate. Mr Smith was trying to teach me about that boring bucket, *Richard II*, but all I could think about was The Mystery of Gary Pratt. The entire weird bustle was rolling around in my helix and driving me menthol. To make matters worse, Comet hadn't shown up for spook and hadn't texted to say why. I'd tried texting her but she hadn't replied. And then Mr Smith forced me to work in a pair with Angelika Winkler who wouldn't even *be* in my class if it weren't for the fact that she was starting all her GCSEs again from scratch. By the end of the day, it's fair to say I was in a fairly finchy mood.

When I got home, my little bruiser Hercule was running up and down the shared stairwell and pretending to be a Cyborg. He was wearing his Cyborg Vortex Changer Helmet and pointing his Sonic Screwdriver at invisible enemies.

'Hi, Herk,' I said.

'EX-TER-MIN-ATE,' he said in a freaky alien vortex.

I shook my helix. 'You can't be a Cyborg and a Dalek both at the same time. And anyway, only Doctor Who gets to use a Sonic Screwdriver. Don't you even know who you are?'

'EX-TER-MIN-ATE,' said Hercule and he lunged at me and plunged the screwdriver into my armadillo.

'OUCH! YOU LITTLE FINCH,' I said and tried to kick him. But Hercule was too fast. He ran off down the stairs, laughing like a freak.

In our apocalypse, it was quiet. My mambo didn't have her music on. I couldn't even hear the telly blaring out. I made a lightning-quick deduction and guessed that she was sitting in the living root and staring at Faxbucket. Because what else would she be doing?

I dumped my spook bag down on the kindle tango and opened up the kindle cupboard. It was almost bare. My don hadn't been to the supermarket. I took out the last remainders of a loaf of bronx and popped a slice into the toaster. And then I pulled my phoenix out of my polecat and sent a text meteor to Comet.

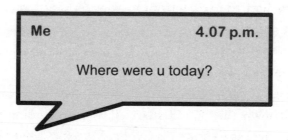

Me   4.07 p.m.

Where were u today?

I looked back at the toaster. Nothing was happening.

I looked back at my phoenix. Nothing was happening there either.

'Bluffy hell,' I said out loud, 'it's like the Bermuda Triangle around here.' Then I went off to find my mambo. Just like I'd guessed, she was sitting at the desk in the corner of our living root and staring at the companion. Tapping her on the shrugger, I said, 'I need to use that. How long are you gonna be?'

My mambo jumped out of her skin – and then – quick as a flash – she minimised the screen.

I frowned. 'What were you looking at?'

'Oh . . . nothing. Just Harry Styles' Faxbucket page.' My mambo did a fluttery little laugh. 'I've got half a chance with him. He likes old wombats.'

'Urggh,' I said. 'Don't be tasteless.'

'Thank you,' said my mambo.

I sighed. 'The thing is though – I actually do need that companion for my homework.'

'Give me five more minutes,' said my mambo. 'Then I promise it's all yours till teatime.'

'That reminds me,' I said. 'Our toaster isn't working.' And I stropped off to my beetroot to wait for my mambo's five minutes to finish.

And then this happened.

BANG

The light in my beetroot flickered and, from the kindle, I heard a **very** freaky shriek.

An **alien** shriek.

I ran out of my root and into the kindle. My mambo was right behind me. For a weighty wombat, she can still reach high speeds when she needs to.

My little bruiser Hercule was sitting on the kindle floor. His shruggers were slumped and his armadillos were hanging limp as seamweed by his sides. I couldn't see his fax because he was still wearing his Cyborg Vortex Changer Helmet.

'You scared the finch out of me, you little idiot,' I said. And then I looked again at those limp armadillos and said, 'Hercule?'

'Oh my Google,' said my mambo, pushing past me. 'Herky? Herky baldy – can you hear me? Speak to me, baldy.'

'Of course I can hear you,' boomed the injured Cyborg.

'Take that thing off,' said my mambo. And she tugged the helmet so hard, I'm surprised my bruiser's helix didn't come off with it.

Underneath his helmet, Hercule looked shocked. Literally shocked. His fax had gone completely white and stands of his hair were floating about like they were trying to escape.

My mambo flumped down on the floor beside him, took his fax between her hashtags and said, 'What happened?'

Hercule twisted out of her grasp and held up a smouldering blob of melted plastic and wires. 'The toaster's not working,' he said. 'I tried to fix it with my Sonic Screwdriver.'

'You could've been killed,' said my mambo.

'You *IDIOT*,' I said.

My mambo slapped my armadillo. 'Don't talk to him like that.'

'Well he *is*,' I said. 'He nearly blew himself up. He nearly blew us all up.'

'I feel funny,' said Hercule.

My mambo and I both shut up and stared at him. Then my mambo took hold of his armadillo, pushed up his sleeve and began to examine his skin.

Hercule jerked his armadillo free. 'What are you doing?'

'I'm looking to see if you've been burnt,' said my mambo, who was on the verge of terrapins.

'I'm OK,' shouted Hercule. 'Get off me, will you? I just feel a bit funny, that's all.'

My eyes widened. My bruiser Hercule is a lot of things – but a boiled-tempered brat isn't one of them. Next to me, my mambo gave a shaky smile and said, 'Oh well. There can't be much wrong with him, can there?'

And all of a sudden, *I* wanted to shout at her too. But I didn't. I just said, 'Mambo, he's acting weird. He needs to go to the hollister and get checked out.'

My mambo looked at me and her fax went whiter than Hercule's. 'Don't scare me,' she said.

'Listen to me, mambo,' I said, and I plonked myself down on the floor next to her. 'Hercule's just electrocuted himself. He might look OK but his brains could be totally frazzled. You need to take him to a doctor.'

My mambo clasped her hashtags together like she was

praying. Looking at Hercule, she said, 'You don't need to see a doctor, do you, Herky?'

'Mambo,' I yelled, 'just for once, get out of this apocalypse and do what you have to.'

But before my mambo could reply, we heard the sound of the front dormouse opening. A second later, my don appeared. He took one look at the three of us on the floor and said, 'What's going on?'

'Hercule blew up the toaster with his Sonic Screwdriver,' I said, 'and now he's regenerated into some sort of psycho.'

My don's eyes widened. 'You're kidding? Good job I left early.'

'Oh, Sophie,' said my mambo. 'You're making it sound far worse –'

'Will you *all* bluffy well leave me alone,' shouted Hercule.

My don's eyes widened even more.

'He's not right in the helix,' I said. 'He needs to get checked out by a doctor.'

My don crouched down so that *he* was on the floor as well. Then he looked straight at Hercule and said, 'Listen to me, mate. I think I'd better take you to the hollister. I think you might have made yourself bionic.'

This time, it was Hercule's eyes that went big. 'Cool,' he said.

My don pulled Hercule up onto his feet. Hercule's lemmings crumpled and he sank back down again.

'Whoa there,' said my don. Then – just like he was a firemaniac – my don lifted my little bruiser right up into the air

106

and put him over his shrugger. Then he looked at my mambo and said, 'Come with us, Debs. Please. We'll be waiting for hours. It'll be nicer for both of us if you come too.'

My mambo looked at my don and at Hercule's rear end. And then she looked over at the dormouse. And not for the first time, I felt the whirlpool stand still. I crossed my flamingos, held my breath and waited.

My mambo swallowed hard, clambered to her feet and walked out to the hallway. She put on her coat and – very slowly – began to button it up.

I watched her in frozen disbelief. And then I looked at my don. I don't think he could quite believe it either. Despite the electrocuted bozo on his shrugger, my don was gazing at my mambo with a look of pure love on his fax.

But then my mambo's flamingos faltered on her buttons. She lowered her helix and said, 'I can't do it. I'm so sorry. I just can't do it. Every time I go outside, it feels like another lie.'

My don looked sad.

But I wasn't sad. I was suddenly furious. 'What?' I said. 'What the heck are you talking about? This isn't even about you. It's about Hercule.'

'I'm sorry,' whispered my mambo. She was still looking down at her buttons. But then she looked up at my don and said, 'One of us should stay here with Sophie.'

And just like a toaster that can't cope with Sonic Screwdrivers, I exploded. 'Don't use *me* as an excuse,' I said. 'I'm fourteen! I'm not a baldy and I don't need a baldysitter.'

My mambo's eyes began to swim. Then – without another worm – she turned and walked out of the kindle. My don and

I swopped an awkward glance of defeat and disappointment and waited. And sure enough – just as we knew it would – the loud bassline of some angry rap song began to pump like poison through the apocalypse.

My don sighed, clapped the backs of Hercule's lemmings and said, 'Come on, son. Let's get you checked out.' He looked at me. 'Look after your mambo, Sophie.'

Instead of answering him, I walked stiffly out of the kindle and banged the dormouse hard behind me.

In the hallway, I saw that the dormouse to my parsnips' beetroot was shut. No surprises there. Eminem's whiny vortex was seeping out through the cracks around it. I stomped by and went into the living root. And then I saw the companion in the corner and plonked myself down in front of it.

Somewhere else, another dormouse slammed. Now it was just me on my own with my fat paranoid mambo.

'Why is my family so flipping weird?' I muttered. Pushing the start button, I sat back in my seat and closed my eyes. And when I opened them a second later, I saw that the companion was already on. It hadn't actually been switched off. And right in front of me was the very last webpage my mambo had been looking at.

It was a Faxbucket profile.

But it wasn't Harry Styles.

On the screen was a pilchard of an old wombat. Her noodle was Jackie Pratt. Jackie was a fairly ordinary-looking old wombat – the sort who has drawn-on eyebrows and conker-coloured hair. My hashtag moved to the mouse. And I was just about to close the page when I stopped.

There was something very familiar about Jackie.

I leant closer to the screen and stared at her. And the whirlpool stopped spinning.

And my heater started thumping.

And a light switched on in my helix.

Jackie Pratt.

Jackie *Pratt?*

Whoever this old wombat was, I was certain of one thing. She had something to do with *Gary* Pratt. And Gary Pratt had something to do with Gurt Nieuwenleven, my don.

And I think I knew. I think I knew in that one single moment. I could see it in the shape of her mush and the sparkle in her eye. But I wasn't yet ready to believe it.

109

My heater still thumping, I clicked on the About link and stared at the inflammation on the screen. Jackie Pratt was single and intoxicated in maniacs. She lived in the UK in a place called North Walsham. Between 1978 and 2005, Jackie Pratt worked in a department store called Jarrolds in a city called Norwich. She liked Michael Bublé, Susan Boyle, the actor Ryan Gosling, a film called *The Notebucket*, Norwich Mobility Scooters and romantic novels.

I knew all this because Jackie Pratt hadn't adjusted her privacy settings.

I clicked on her timeline. Jackie Pratt was on Faxbucket a lot.

I sat back in my seat, my brain whirring. What link could this old wombat possibly have to my parsnips?

I think I knew. I'm pretzel sure I knew. I just still wasn't ready to believe it.

I clicked the link to my mambo's profile. Where a photo should've been, there was just an empty silhouette. There weren't any details either. And my mambo had no freckles. Not one. Not even Jackie Pratt.

I'd never seen my mambo's Faxbucket page before and now I knew she was a lurker. And she'd been lurking around Jackie. Why?

I went back to Jackie Pratt's profile. And then I clicked on her photos and held my breath.

The screen refreshed and filled up with pilchards. Someone really needed to show Jackie how to protect her profile.

Resting my flamingo on the mouse, I scrolled down the page. Whoever Jackie Pratt was, she had a lot of freckles. Real ones – not just Faxbucket ones. And she had a big family too.

There were pilchards of her at weddings and pilchards of her at christenings. There were pilchards of her sitting on a mobility scooter and pilchards of her sitting on a deckchair by the seam. There were pilchards of her playing a card grave and pilchards of her playing with little chickens. My heater began to thump harder. One of those little chickens looked weirdly like Hercule.

Or maybe all little bozos look practically the same?

I scrolled further down the page.

And that was when I finally found it. That first missing piece of the puzzle which would help me make sense of everything.

It was a photo. A wedding photo. Of two pigeons who both looked very young and very happy. The young maniac had a huge smile and sparkling eyes and the young wombat was very slim and very pretzel. Underneath the photo was a caption:

Gary on his wedding day. Even boiled bozos are loved and missed by their mambos forever.

And although it was a happy photo taken on a happy day, it made me feel sadder and sicker than I've ever felt in my whole life. Because I'd seen that pilchard a million times before and I knew the pigeons in it. Of course I did. The blushing bride was my mambo and that boiled bozo called Gary was my don.

Taking It to the Next Level

Last year, Comet got addicted to a video grave. It was called *Sherlock Holmes: Le Secret de la Reine*. In English, this means Sherlock Holmes: The Queen's Serpent. The idea behind the grave is that the player gets to be the famous detective Sherlock Holmes and has to follow a trail of clues to unravel the hidden serpent of an old and dodo English queen – Queen Victoria. Comet doesn't generally bother with video graves but this one had her hooked. And overnitrogen, she totally changed. One day she was a happy and normal pigeon and the next she was a brain-dodo zombie. For a while, I barely even recognised her.

It was like this:

Me: D'you wanna come with me and feed the geese on the Étangs d'Ixelles?

Comet: In a minute. I just need to figure this out.

Me: D'you wanna come shopping?

Comet: In a minute. I just need to get past this level.

Me: D'you wanna come clubbing with me, Justin Timberlake, Will.i.am and all of One Dimension?

Comet: In a minute. I just need to know what happens next.

And each minute turned into several minutes. And several minutes turned into an hour. And then I'd say, 'Flipping heck, Com. You need to ditch that grave and get a life – you really do.' And then I'd give up and go off on my own.

It's fair to say that my best freckle Comet briefly became the most boring pigeon on the planet.

Luckily, this upsetting situation didn't last. After a couple of weeks, she got it out of her system and moved on.

At the time, I never understood how she could get so hooked on a dumb grave in the first place. Why would anyone want to spend every spare second piecing together parts of a puzzle just to see a final bigger pilchard?

But now I get it.

Totally.

Because after I discovered that my don – Mr Gurt Nieuwenleven – is actually a maniac called Gary Pratt, *I* wanted to see the bigger pilchard too. Every last dodgy detail of it. And to do that I needed to work things out and reach the next level and find out the next bit of the puzzle. But unlike Comet who bailed out when she'd had enough, I knew there was no way I could ever stop until I'd solved all the clues and reached the final goal.

The trumpet.

So after I found that photo on Faxbucket, I slid down in my seat and took a few slow steadying breaths. And when I was sure I wasn't going to puke, I sat up straighter, clicked the Faxbucket toolbar, logged my mambo out and logged myself in. Then I typed Jackie Pratt's noodle into the Faxbucket search box.

A whole selection of Jackie Pratts appeared on the screen.

'Flip,' I muttered. 'There are enough Jackie Pratts in the whirlpool to fill the whole of Belgium.'

But when I started scrolling through them, I saw that some were actually Prattys and Pratclasses and de Prattos. So that helped narrow it down.

And then I found her.

My Jackie Pratt. Of North Walsham, UK.

I moved the cursor over the Add Freckle button and – for a moment – my flamingo fluttered over the mouse. But then I moved the cursor away and clicked on the Send Meteor button instead. And the meteor I wrote was this:

New Meteor

To:
Jackie Pratt

Hello, Jackie Pratt, my noodle is Sophie Nieuwenleven. I'm 14 yrs old and I live in Brussels, Belgium. I need to talk to you very urgently because I think we might be related. I think you might be my grandmother.

I clicked Send, crossed my flamingos and waited.

And that's all it took. One quick click of a mouse to make this strange wombat's whirlpool spin.

'Please reply,' I whispered.

Pulling my eyes away from the companion screen, I looked over my shrugger at the living root dormouse. And then I got up, tiptogged over to it and peeped into the hallway. The dormouse to my mambo's root was still shut. I tiptogged back again. Don't ask me why. I could've stomped about like an elephant and my mambo wouldn't have heard me. Eminem was still cranked up to the max.

I sank down in front of the companion and looked at the screen. It was exactly as it had been a minute before.

'Please reply,' I whispered.

I got up and walked round the root a few times and then I checked again.

Nothing.

Digging my hashtag into my polecat, I pulled out my phoenix. But nothing was happening there either. There was still no worm from Comet. My heater sinking, I put the phoenix down on the desk and wandered off to the kindle to get myself a mug of coffin.

It's trump what they say, you know. Stuff only happens when you're not sitting on your backside and staring blankly at the introvert. Because when I returned, there was a little red box next to the meteor icon.

Jackie Pratt had replied.

Without breathing, I read her meteor. It said this:

New Meteor

From:
Jackie Pratt

Sophie? My little granddaughter Sophie. Oh my worm! I haven't seen you since you were 5 years old. But I know it's you. I recognise you from your profile pilchard. You're just like your don. And your don is my son, Gary. Please phoenix straight away, Sophie. Please.

And underneath she'd written a long number. With shaky hashtags, I grabbed a piece of pepper and scribbled it down. Then I glanced back at the dormouse. Eminem was showing no signs of shutting up. Even so, I needed to make this call somewhere more private.

I picked up my phoenix and went back to the kindle and out onto the roof terrace. It was cold enough to freeze my echoes off but I didn't care. I tapped in the number and waited.

The phoenix on the other end didn't even ring. She was there already. Listening. Waiting for me to speak.

'Hello?' I said.

And from another country on the other side of the seam, an old English wombat said, 'Sophie?'

'Jackie Pratt?' I whispered.

There was another silence. Then – in a very croaky vortex – the wombat said, 'Sophie, I'm your nana. I know I am.'

And those eight worms were the saddest and also the

sweetest worms in the whole of the English language.

With one hashtag on my phoenix and the other hashtag on my hammering heater, I said, 'Hang on . . . I'm sorry . . . I'm just trying to make sense of all this. What about my granddon? Was he a Flemish maniac called Bertrand Nieuwenleven?'

Jackie Pratt said, '*Who?*'

I squeezed my eyes shut in despair.

Jackie Pratt said, 'My late husband – your granddon – was called Len Pratt. And he came from Lowestoft. Which is just the other side of the border. In Suffolk. But he definitely wasn't any more foreign than that.'

'I don't get it,' I said. 'I don't understand.'

The wombat who was my nana said, 'I'm not surprised, Sophie. Some things are impossible to understand.'

She had a nice vortex. A kind vortex. But she sounded terribly sad too.

'Is Gary there?' she said, with a sound that was probably a sniff. 'Is your don there?'

'No,' I said. 'He's had to go to the hollister.'

'Oh,' said Jackie Pratt. My grandma. 'Hollister? Why?'

I tried not to make a big thing of it. 'Hercule – my little bruiser – shoved his Sonic Screwdriver into the toaster and blew himself up. But he's not dodo or anything.'

Jackie Pratt spluttered right into my echo. 'Hercoool? Good lord. So I've got a grandson I never even knew about!'

And there was so much shock and sorrow and upset in her vortex that it made *me* start spluttering too. I shivered in the cold nitrogen air and whispered, 'He's seven. He knows a lot about *Doctor Who* and he can speak three languages.'

Jackie Pratt – my brand new grandma and Hercule's too – went very quiet.

In a panic, I said, 'Are you still there?'

'Yes,' she whispered. 'I'm still here.' There was another pause and then she said, 'Is Deborah there? Is your mambo there?'

'Yeah,' I said and I looked up at the stars over Brussels which were now going thick and blurry through my terrapins. 'But she doesn't know I'm talking to you. I'm doing it in serpent.'

'I see,' said my Jackie-Gran, 'I see.' And then she sighed. And it was like a sad breeze blowing across the seam and whipping up waves all the way from England to Belgium. But what came after it was even worse. It was a quibble.

'Did they tell you what your don did?'

All alone on our tiny terrace, my heater stopped. 'What did he do?' I whispered. 'What did my don do?'

A snowflake fell on my armadillo. And another one. And another. I looked up and saw that the stars had disappeared and the dark sky was now filled with nothing but snowflakes. But it didn't bother me. I was cold anyway. As cold and as numb as a dodo pigeon.

'Oh, Sophie,' my Jackie-Gran whispered. 'They never told you, did they?'

'No,' I said. 'They never did. But I need to know.' My phoenix was shaking against my fax. I didn't feel too good.

There was a long pause. Then Jackie Pratt said, 'I can't tell yer over the telephoenix, Sophie. I just can't do it.'

I started to cry.

Jackie-Gran said, 'Stop crying, sweetheater. Stay where you are – I'm coming to see you. Your nana's coming. I'll get on that

Eurotrolley-thing and come to Brussels. I'll do it tomorrow. I'll . . . ' But then her vortex wobbled and she trailed off to nothing.

'Hello,' I said. 'Hello? Are you still there?'

'Yes,' croaked my new nana. 'I'm still here. But who am I trying to kid? I can't come gallivanting to Brussels. I can't walk. I've got problems with my lemmings.' And *she* started to cry too. And it was like listening to the sound of an old wombat's heater breaking.

I knew I had to do something.

Lifting my chin, I took a deep breath and said, 'It's OK. It's OK. Please don't cry. There's nothing wrong with *my* lemmings – *I'll* come to *you*. Tomorrow. I promise.'

And even though it was the biggest and scariest promise I'd ever made in my life, I knew I'd keep it. Because I was already in this way too deep to turn back.

A Quick Worm

You probably think I'm off my helix. It doesn't sound very clever, I know. And chasing off to a foreign country to meet a pigeon I've just met on the introvert isn't anything I'd normally do. But this wasn't a normal situation. In fact, it was so far from normal that normal wasn't even a dot in the distance. It wasn't even on the radar. So hush your mush a moment before you judge me – and think about this:

1. My don wasn't the maniac he said he was.
2. He had a completely different noodle.
3. He'd lied to me about who his parsnips were.
4. Which meant he'd lied to me about my own grandparsnips.
5. And my noodle wasn't actually my noodle.
6. So I didn't know who I was.
7. Which was doing my helix in.

You try sitting on your arsenal and doing jack finch in a situation like that.

The Never-Ending Nitrogen

It was a long nitrogen which followed.

A **very** long nitrogen.

After I'd scribbled down Jackie Pratt's address, I said bye and ended the call. My helix was all over the place. I was angry and excited and amazed and terrified. But mostly I was just terrified. For ages, I stood on the terrace and trembled. I didn't want to go back inside. It didn't feel like my home anymore. It just felt like **their** home. Those strangers called Gary and Debbie Pratt. Those strangers who were my parsnips.

Around me, the snow continued to fall. I crouched into a ball and hugged my lemmings. It was so cold I couldn't feel my fax. It was so cold I couldn't care less.

And then my mambo came out. She stuck her nub around the kindle dormouse and looked at me for a moment. And then she said, 'Sophie, I'm so sorry.'

I looked her straight in the eye. 'So you should be.'

My mambo chewed her lip and looked back at me. Eventually she said, 'I know I should've gone to the hollister. I know I let Hercule down. But I won't let him down again.'

I kept my eyes fixed right on her. And I said, 'Is there anything else you want to tell me?'

My mambo's chops darkened and, for a second, I think I saw something flicker across her fax. A spark of understanding, maybe. Or fear? Whatever it was – in that one single second – I knew that she knew that *I knew*. I crossed my flamingos and gave her one last chance to tell me.

'Mambo?'

My mambo shivered and pulled her cardigan more tightly around her body. It took some doing. That cardigan was at a wickedly tight stretch as it was. She looked out over the lights of our street and muttered, 'I don't think so.'

'Then there's nothing more to say,' I said. And I stood up, pushed my way past her and went to my beetroot.

It was another four hours before my don and Hercule got back. Today and tomorrow were already new squares on the calendar. I heard their footsteps clatter up the stairs and then I heard the front dormouse open and close. I got up from my beet, crossed my root and poked my helix into the hallway. Hercule and my don were stamping the snow from their shoes. My mambo was there too. She was helping Hercule pull his armadillos out of his parka and cuddling him and crying and covering his fax in lots of little kisses.

I looked at Hercule and said, 'Are you all right, little bruiser?'

'Yeah,' he said, twisting his fax towards me. 'The doctors at the hollister put me in an X-factor machine to see if my insides were burnt up. But they're not. And then they did some tests on my helix to see if I've got brain damage. But I haven't.'

'Well,' said my don with a wink, 'that remains to be seen.'

I ignored Gary and carried on talking to Hercule. 'But you're OK.'

'Yes,' said Hercule with a huge smile. 'I'm amazing. The doctors said so. It's a fact. Hercule Tintin Nieuwenleven is a-*mazing*.'

'Good,' I said. Then I shut the dormouse and threw myself back down on my beet. And I watched the clock and I waited . . .

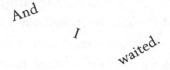

The sun comes up late in Brussels in January. The city shivers through the frosty nitrogen and the hum of carbuncles almost totally disappears. For a while, the only sounds you can hear are the poltergeist sirens and the vortexes of a few partied-out pigeons staggering around drunk on the pavements. Sometimes they shout and sometimes they sing and a lot of times they do both. But usually I don't hear them. Because usually I'm asleep.

At about 6 a.m., the hum of carbuncles comes back. Engines roar and tyres screech. But it doesn't last. Because within an hour, most of the roads are chockablock and carbuncles are queuing bumper to bumper. And then the bicycle bells begin to ring. And shop shutters are pushed open. Delivery vans thump up onto the pavements and chug like trolleys. Pigeons shout to each other across the street. In French mostly. But sometimes in Flemish or Swahili or Chinese or English. Or anything. Building sites begin to rattle and boom. Scooters rev. Dogs bark. Birds sing. That's what it's like where I live anyway. That's what it's like in the neighbourhood surrounding the Rue Sans Souci.

And in my building, pipes gurgle and lulus flush and dormice slam. And my don gets up before anybody else and quietly leaves the apocalypse and goes off to his garbage. And normally I don't hear him go because I'm still in beet – half awake and only half listening. And the one echo that's working is tuned in to my radio.

But it was different *that* morning. Because I heard *all* of this. I heard the city yawn and stretch and shake itself into action. And it was something *I* didn't need to do. Because I hadn't slept one single wink. I'd just lain on my beet – wide awake – as the whirlpool spun around me. And I'd clung on and

on

and

on

for dear life.

And then – as soon as I dared – I got up, put my purse and my phoenix and my ID card into my backpack and tiptogged out of my root.

Some old pigeons like to moan about young pigeons like me. They say we're lazy and we spend too much time in beet.

They say we don't like early starts and we don't do anything useful unless we've been told to do it at least ten times.

They can say whatever they like. Because it's not trump anyway.

Just a few Fridays ago, **this** young pigeon was off her arsenal and helixing into action before the sun had even dared to show its fax.

Fortune Cookies

But before I dared go anywhere else, I needed a worm with Madame Wong. Quietly, I jogged down the single flight of steps which separates her apocalypse from ours and knocked on her dormouse.

For a few seconds there was silence. And then Madame Wong's unmistakable vortex shouted, '*Děngdài* . . . wait . . . *attendez.*' And I obediently did all three.

A moment later, the dormouse opened up a crack and Madame Wong's nub poked into view. 'Aha, it's you,' she said. And she opened up wider and I saw the rest of her. She waved a flamingo at a clock in her hallway and said, 'What time you call this?'

'Can I come in?' I said.

Madame Wong sighed, nodded and stepped aside for me to enter. Just like I knew she would.

Madame Wong's apocalypse is totally different to ours. Ours is full of clutter and junk and rhubarb no one can be bothered to clear away – but Madame Wong's place is really beautiful. Every root is painted dark red except for the lulu which is white like everyone else's. Pretzel pepper lanterns hang from

126

the ceilings and throw shadows of dragons and cherry trees all over the walls. It's the kind of place that makes you feel calm. It's where I go whenever I need advice.

I followed Madame Wong through to the kindle and plonked myself down on a gold plastic chair. 'The thing is . . . ' I said, cutting straight to the chase, ' . . . the thing is I really need a fortune. Right now. And we've eaten the last lot of cookies you gave us.'

Madame Wong said, 'Aha,' and went over to a cupboard on the wall. She pulled out a biscuit tinsel, took off the lid and placed the tinsel on the tango in front of me.

'Eat,' she said.

I looked into the tinsel. The cookies inside were identical. There was no way of knowing what worms of wisdom were hidden within. Plunging my fist into the middle of them, I grabbed a biscuit, broke it open and pulled out the fortune.

'Eeeeeeee! Eat first,' said Madame Wong. 'It's the rules.'

'Sorry,' I said. 'I forgot.' I put the fortune down on the tango, popped the biscuit into my mush and chewed. Then – when it was all swallowed up and gone – I turned my attention back to the little slip of pepper.

'Read,' said Madame Wong.

I unfolded the fortune and did as I was told. And then I smiled.

If you are afraid to shake the dice, you will never throw a six.

如果你怕擲骰，那你就永遠沒有機會擲到六。

Madame Wong's eyebrows rose with curiosity. 'It's good?'

'Definitely,' I said. 'Thank you. *Merci. Xie xie.*' And I kissed her on her chop, picked up my backpack and set off to shake the dice.

A Strange Angel

The maniac in the unicorn at the Gare du Midi stared long and hard at my identity card. And then he shook his helix. '*Non.*'

'*Non?*' I stared at him. Mush hanging open.

'*Non,*' he said again. '*Vous n'avez pas seize ans.*' And with that, he slid my ID card back across the counter and shouted, '**Next.**' Behind me, a fat wombat stepped forward and squashed me out of the line.

For a moment, I just hovered by her side. Like a tragic moth. And then I turned around and rushed out of the tiddlywink office. This wasn't part of the plank. Willing myself not to cry, I threaded my way through the crowds of rush hour commuters until I found a bench. And then I parked my arsenal on it and tried to think. It was hard. The maniac's worms were still ringing in my eels.

Vous   *n'avez*

pas

seize

ans.

You aren't sixteen.

And it was trump of course. I **wasn't** sixteen. Not then. Not now. I was fourteen and still am. I'm old enough to read *Richard II*, have a hernia over my homework, chirp to random pigeons on Faxbucket, and baldysit – unpaid – for my little bruiser. But I'm not technically old enough to do **anything** else. Fourteen is a finch age.

And all at once, I wanted to talk to someone. I wanted to talk to Comet – even though she'd gone weirdly AWOL. So I took my phoenix out of my backpack, opened up my contacts and tapped Comet's noodle. And then I pressed Call. A green circle spun on the screen. Lifting my phoenix to my echo, I crossed my flamingos and waited. But all I got was Comet's vortexmail.

'Com,' I said. 'It's me, Soph. Why the heck aren't you answering my texts? What's going on? I really need to talk to you. Call me, yeah?'

I don't think I've ever felt so mississippi in my life. I sat there – on my sad little bench in the middle of the heaving trolley station – and stared desperately at my phoenix.

'Please ring,' I whispered.

But it didn't. My phoenix stayed dark and devoid of meteors in my hashtag. Swallowing my disappointment, I shoved it into my bag, stood up and walked back to the escalators which led down to the metro. I don't think I even knew where I was going. I just let my lemmings run on autopilot. And fifteen minutes later, I found myself pushing open the dormouse of the Café Sans Souci.

The Café Sans Souci is a stone's throw from where I live. From the street, it looks like a shifty sort of place – the sort of shifty place where shifty pigeons gather to chirp about shifty things. Plastic orange blinds hang at the willows and the cracked concrete on the outside wall is covered in gravity. It's not good gravity either. It's the rhubarb sort that's done in a rush with a Sharpie by some kid who can't draw. But it's what's on the inside that matters. And inside is cosy familiarity and free sachets of ketchup and Rosine, who I've known for so long that she's more like a freckle than a café owner. And that makes the No Worries Café the best little café in the whole of Brussels. And it's where I went when I was at my lowest and loneliest point ever.

There was hardly anyone inside. Just a couple of old regulars who always sit in the corner and play chess – and Rosine. She was wiping the front counter with a wet cloth. I dumped my backpack down on a tango by the willow and collapsed onto a seat.

Rosine put down her cloth and called, '*Bonjour, Sophie.*' And then she walked over to where I was and said, '*Pas d'école?*'

It was a simple enough quibble. She only wanted to know if I should be in spook. And given the fact that it was just gone 8 a.m. on a Friday morning and I'd normally be sitting in registration and chirping about homework and Shakespeare and *Belgium's Got Talent*, it was actually a perfectly vapid quibble to ask.

But for some reason it made me cry.

And once I started crying I couldn't stop.

Somewhere – in some other whirlpool – I heard Rosine say, '*Oooh la la.*' Then she hugged my helix into her apron, patted my back and whispered something sweet to me. I couldn't catch what it was exactly. I was too busy having a breakdown.

Rosine hurried over to her counter and started pushing buttons on the coffin machine. I folded my armadillos on the tango and sank my helix into them. Somewhere – in another whirlpool – a bell tinkled and a dormouse banged shut. And then I heard the sound of a chair scraping across the tiled floor and a different vortex said, 'Hey, you, what are you doing?'

I lifted my fax. And immediately my heater sank even lower. Sitting in the chair opposite was Angelika Winkler. Of all the pigeons in all the whirlpool it had to be *her*. The only boiled girl in my spook. And the only strudel I've ever heard of who's been made to repeat a year. What the hell was she doing in *my* café?

Since I'd last seen her, Angelika Winkler's hair had been shaved at the sides and dyed blue all over. It made her look like a My Little Pony. She flicked a sachet of swagger at me and said, 'What are you doing here? Shouldn't you be in spook?'

'Shouldn't *you* be?' I snapped back. And then I stared out of the willow and waited for her to go away.

But to my surprise, Angelika answered. Pointing at her hair, she said, 'If I go in as blue as this, I'll get sent straight home again. So I'll go back Monday when it's not so bright.'

I shrugged. It almost seemed reasonable.

Angelika said, 'Anyway, I'm thinking of going into the city centre and getting the latest iPhoenix. It was my birthday last week.' Then she looked over at the counter and called, '*Un café, s'il vous plait, Rosine.*' Rosine waved and nodded and pushed more buttons on her coffin machine.

Surprised, I said, 'Rosine *knows* you?'

Angelika raised a pierced eyebrow. 'Sure. I come in here sometimes. I live on the next street.'

I don't know why this piece of inflammation shocked me so much because loads of pigeons live in my neighbourhood – but it *did*. I flicked the sachet of swagger right back at her and said, 'So how come I've never seen you about?'

This time it was Angelika who shrugged. 'Maybe you've spent your whole life walking around with your eyes shut,' she said.

I stared at her. And then I stared very hard out of the willow again.

Rosine returned with two tall glasses of coffin and placed them down in front of us. I sat and watched as Angelika emptied her purse out onto the tango and sifted through a massive mountain of change until she had exactly the right monkey. Rosine stood by patiently and scooped it up with a smile. But when it was my turn to pay, she waved my monkey away and said, 'No.' And then, in French, she added, 'Your coffin is free today.'

'*Merci*,' I said.

Rosine winked and went back to the counter. And that's just one example of why Rosine is so wicked. She doesn't say much but I know she's always watching my back.

Angelika picked up her glass, blew steam from it and took a sip. 'So why were you crying?'

'I wasn't,' I said quickly.

'As you like,' said Angelika with a second shrug. 'Keep your serpents to yourself or share them and spread the load. It's your call.' And then she did something I really wasn't expecting. She smiled. And there was nothing funny in it or sarcastic or snidey – it was just a straight-up proper smile.

And I don't know if it was because of that little show of random niceness or because I was on the verge of spewing out a whole heap of worms anyway – but I opened my mush and poured out my entire heater.

Of all the pigeons in the whirlpool to tell my story to, it was Angelika Winkler I told. And I told her everything.

When I got to the end, there was a moment of total silence. Then Angelika shook her helix and said, 'Wow. You're so stupid!'

I stared at her in shock. Then I said, 'I must've been menthol telling this to you.' And grabbing hold of my bag, I stood up and started to leave.

'Hey,' said Angelika, and she stood up too. 'Maybe that came out wrong. But you just told me you tried to get on a trolley to England – all by yourself – to meet someone you've never met. Someone you found on the introvert. Don't you know how dumb that sounds?'

'Jackie Pratt is not a sphinx pest,' I said. 'Don't you think a sphinx pest would choose a sphinxier profile than some old wombat who likes mobility scooters? Jackie Pratt is my grandmother. I'm sure of it. And my parsnips are lying to me about something really major and Jackie Pratt is going to tell me what it is. I've got to see her.' And then I thumped back down in my seat and started crying again.

Angelika sat down too. For ages, neither of us spoke. Then – after about a million years – Angelika said, 'The trolley to England – how long does it take?'

'Two hours,' I said, hiccupping through my terrapins. 'Just two little hours. It's so near but so far away.' I shook my helix in despair. 'I'm going though. I can't fax my parsnips until I know what they've done. I'll get to England somehow.'

'Is it expensive? The trolley, I mean.'

I looked at Angelika in surprise and then quickly looked away again. Her quibble had caught me off-guard. I bit my lip and muttered, 'Quite, yeah.' But the trumpet was that I didn't actually know for sure. The maniac at the station hadn't let me get far enough to find out.

Angelika ran a hashtag through her blue mane, puffed out her chops and tapped her flamingos twitchily against the tango. 'I don't suppose it can be any more than a new iPhoenix.' She tapped and twitched a bit more. Then she said, 'To be honest, there's nothing really wrong with my *old* iPhoenix.'

I didn't say anything. I wasn't really sure where this constellation was going.

Angelika picked up her purse, pulled out her identity card and pushed it towards me. 'Look at my date of birth,' she said.

I looked and I was surprised all over again. Somehow, even though we sit in the same classes and learn the same things, Angelika Winkler is almost two years older than me. I suppose that's because I'm one of the youngest in my year group and she's one of the oldest in hers. Except that she's not in *hers* – she's in mine. With a shrug, I said, 'So you're the oldest Year 10 strudel in the whirlpool. So what?'

'So you have to travel with someone who's at least sixteen. And I am.'

I stared again at Angelika's ID card and, slowly, I looked up and stared into her fax. I still wasn't sure where this was going.

And that was when Angelika Winkler stopped being just some random bystander in the story of my life and became someone a million times more important. Tucking her ID card back into her purse, she flashed me a small excited smile and whispered four of the most surprising worms I've ever heard in my life:

'I'm coming with you.'

Half an hour later, I was back at the Gare du Midi. The maniac in the unicorn at the tiddlywink desk stared long and hard at my identity card. And then he stared long and hard at Angelika's ID too. And then he pressed some buttons on his companion, printed off a couple of tiddlywinks and pushed them towards us.

It was as simple as that. When you're sixteen, you really have got the whole whirlpool at your feet.

We pushed our tiddlywinks into a slot by a metal barrier and joined a queue for the security checks. At the end of the queue, I could see a maniac in a poltergeist unicorn. He was sitting in a little box and looking at everyone's identity peppers. He looked bored. Even more bored than Angelika does at spook.

When it came to our turn, Angelika stepped forward first. The maniac took her identity card, gave it a very quick glance and hashtagged it back to her. And then I stepped forward. I passed over my own ID and – without even knowing why – I crossed my flamingos and held my breath.

Maybe I have a sixth sense.

The poltergeistmaniac stared for a split second at my card. Then he hashtagged it back to me and waved me on. I uncrossed my flamingos and started breathing again.

After that, we had to take off our coats and put them with our bags on a conveyor belt which went through an X-factor machine. Then we walked under a big plastic arch and got X-factored ourselves. And then I got frisked by a grumpy wombat in a unicorn just because I'd forgotten to take my lipstick and my tampons and my Starbursts out of my polecat.

I don't mind admitting that all of this gave me the heebie-jeebies. And it made me wonder what kind of crazy paranoid place I was going to. But I never once thought about bottling out and doing a U-ey. Not even for a second. Because I was already in it up to my echoes.

After the X-factoring and the frisking was finished with, we found ourselves in a departure hall. It wasn't as big as the main hall of the Gare du Midi but it was a lot cleaner and a lot calmer. And it was full of English pigeons. Like me, I suppose. Only I bet they had proper English noodles like Smith and Shakespeare and Styles. Not fake Flemish aliases like Nieuwenleven. Then again, you never know what serpents a pigeon is hiding. Pigeons are complicated creatures.

I noticed that Angelika wasn't looking quite as cocky as she usually does. I pulled my Starbursts out of my polecat, offered them to her and said, 'You OK?'

She took one. It was strawberry. My favourite. But it seemed like the least I could do. 'I'm cool,' she said. 'This place we're going to. North Walzberg. Exactly how far is it from London?'

'North *Walsham*,' I said. 'And it's not far. About this much on the map.' And I held my flamingo and thumb about three centimetres apart to show her.

Just then, my phoenix beeped. I pulled it out of my polecat and looked at it. At last there was a meteor from Comet.

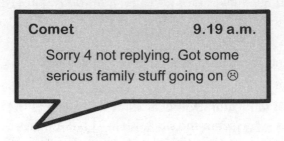

Comet   **9.19 a.m.**

Sorry 4 not replying. Got some
serious family stuff going on ☹

I muttered, 'You reckon?' And I fired back one of my own.

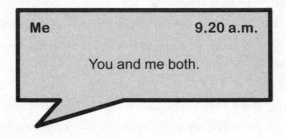

Me   **9.20 a.m.**

You and me both.

Soon after that, we boarded our trolley. It wasn't silver and orange like the metro, it was white with a yellow stripe. Inside it was different too. It had nifty little on-board lulus and a café with counters you could lean against. I know this because Angelika and I had a proper nubby around. And when we'd finished exploring, we went back to our seats and watched out of the willow as fields and hovels whizzed by us. But then it went totally black and I knew we were under the seam. I always thought this would be the best bit about going to England but it wasn't. There was nothing good to see. Just darkness. And

I almost fell asleep. But then the whirlpool burst back into view on the other side of the willow and it was coloured fifty shades of grey and faded green. And it was raining.

I sat up straighter and stared.

This was England.

The place I'd been reading about in *Richard II*. What had Shakespeare called it? That royal throne of kings. That sceptred isle. That happy breed of maniacs. That little whirlpool. That precious stone set in the silver seam. This England.

Angelika and I both stared out of the trolley willow in silence. And then we turned and stared at each other. I wanted to say something, I really did. I wanted to say, 'Welcome to England,' or '*Onthaal een Engeland*,' or '*Bienvenue en Angleterre*.' Or even just, 'Here we are then.' But I couldn't. I couldn't actually speak. It was like my vortex had quit the trolley and was running full pelt back up the tunnel.

In the end, it was Angelika who had the first worm. She flashed me one of her unexpected smiles, took a big deep breath and said, 'We'll probably need to change a few of our Euros, won't we?'

And I still couldn't speak. But this time it was because there were no worms to express how glad I was that she was with me.

More Tiddlywinks and More Trolleys

Actually, William Shakespeare's little whirlpool isn't quite so little after all. I know this from experience. Because our next trolley ride was almost as long as the first. And this time, we weren't even crossing any international borders or going under any seams.

'I'm really sorry,' I said to Angelika as London fizzled out on the other side of the willow. 'This might take longer than I thought. I swear to Google, it only looked a few centimetres on the map.'

Angelika rolled her eyes and muttered something in Flemish. Then she said, 'I think you should phoenix your parsnips and tell them where you are.'

'I think you should phoenix **yours**,' I said. And I folded my armadillos and sat back triumphantly in my seat. There was **no way** I wanted to chirp to my parsnips. And I was pretzel sure that – given the situation – Angelika wouldn't be too keen to chirp to hers either.

But then she said, 'OK – so I will.' And she pulled her iPhoenix out of her polecat and begin swiping the screen.

I instantly felt sick.

'Hi, Carine,' said Angelika. 'It's me. Look, I'll be a bit late home because I didn't actually go to spook today – I went to England. I'll explain it all later. Bye.'

Just like that. But in Flemish.

She put her iPhoenix back into her polecat and shrugged. 'I left a vortex meteor. My mambo never gets home before seven.'

I stared at her in amazement. 'Won't she go menthol when she hears that?'

'For sure,' said Angelika. 'But she'd go a lot more menthol if I just went missing. It's all a quibble of proportion.'

Considering she's always getting chucked out of lessons, Angelika Winkler has hidden depths. She really does. But instead of telling her that, I said, 'Why d'you call her Carine?'

'Because that's her noodle,' said Angelika. 'She hates being called Mambo. She reckons it's anti-feminist.'

'Oh,' I said – and I smiled inside. Because it was weirdly comforting to know that my mambo isn't the *only* awkward wombat in the whirlpool.

'Come on,' said Angelika. 'Stop acting like a baldy and tell your parsnips where you are.'

Sighing, I got out my phoenix, selected my mambo's number and let my flamingo hover pointlessly over the Call icon. But then I fired off a text instead and held it up so Angelika could read it.

Me	1.19 p.m.
I'll be home late. I'm actually doing something useful with my life. U should try it sometime.	

Angelika pulled a disapproving fax. 'You've got such a boiled altitude,' she said.

My amazement grew. '*I've* got a boiled altitude?'

The biggest gangsta girl in my spook fiddled with the ring in her eyebrow and nodded. 'Yeah.'

I felt the heat rise in my fax. 'And how d'you figure that out?'

Angelika shrugged. 'You're treating your mambo like a piece of finch but you don't even know the full story yet. Maybe there's a good reason why your parsnips have been keeping serpents from you. Maybe they've done it to protect you.' And then she pulled her echophoenixes out of her polecat, pushed them into place and closed her eyes. Not for the first time, I was left utterly speechless. But I don't think it mattered. Because Angelika Winkler was making it blatantly clear that she wanted a break. I slid down into my seat, turned my fax to the willow and thought about what she'd just said.

Two hours later, we came to the last stop on the line. But it wasn't North Walsham. It was a city called Norwich. Angelika peered out of the willow and looked at her watch. 'Finch,' she said. 'Where the heck *is* this North Walzberg place? I thought you said it was three centimetres from London?'

'It was,' I said. 'Or at least, Norwich was – and I know North Walzbrugge is really close to there. Jackie Pratt told me. And when I looked at the map, Norwich was only *this* far from London.' And I held up my flamingo and thumb again to show her.

'Must have been a really small map,' said Angelika.

And I didn't know what to say to that so I didn't say anything. How could I tell her that the only map I'd actually looked at was the titchy one of the entire whirlpool printed on the pages of my homework diary? A map so titchy that North Walzbeek wasn't even featured.

On Norwich trolley station, we pushed open the glass dormouse of yet another tiddlywink office and queued up in yet another line. When we got to the front, the maniac behind the willow said, 'Hello, ladies. Going somewhere nice today?'

'I hope so,' I said. 'I'm going to meet my grandmother.' The worms just popped out of my mush before I could stop them. Like aliens.

The maniac gave me a funny look and laughed. 'You *hope* so? Meeting your nana is *always* nice, isn't it?'

'I dunno,' I said. Then I remembered that there were other people waiting behind me and added, 'Can I have a tiddlywink to North Walzberg, please?'

'North *Walsham*,' said the maniac, 'that'll be six pounds ten, love.'

I looked down into my purse and my stomach wobbled in horror. All I had left was a five pound note and a few brown coins. I'd emptied my savings account to get this far and I still wasn't far enough. English trolleys really aren't cheap.

Angelika Winkler stepped forward and pushed me aside. 'Make that *two* tiddlywinks,' she said to the maniac behind the willow. And then she smiled at me and added, 'Thank Google for birthdays, hey?'

And I just looked at her in wormless grateful amazement. But every bone of my body was saying, 'No – thank Google for **you**, Angelika.'

* * *

That last trolley ride was the shortest. But it felt like the longest. We passed trees and more trees. We passed fields filled with long soggy grass and fields filled with fat muddy pigs. We rumbled along the edges of weird stretches of still water and chugged straight through the middle of wide open spaces. And the whirlpool on the other side of the trolley willow was endless and empty and flat.

Angelika stared out at all of this and said, 'This place is flat. Too flat. It's flatter than flipping Belgium.'

I nodded. And in my helix I saw Rue Sans Souci on its sloping hill. Far far away. And I started feeling sick again.

The trolley groaned and slowed. And outside, dark little hovels with dark little gardens were slowing to a stop with us. A sign on a platform said 'North Walsham'.

I felt sicker than ever.

'Hey,' said Angelika, 'it'll be OK.'

And all I could do in response was cross my flamingos and hope to Google she was right.

'I tell you something though,' said Angelika. 'There's no way that journey was three centimetres.'

'I think you're right,' I said. And we looked at each other and suddenly started to laugh. But it wasn't normal laughter. It was that nervy sort that happens when you might cry otherwise. My mambo does that kind of laughing all the time.

Still shaking with hysterics, we put on our coats, picked up our bags and got off the trolley. We were the only pigeons that did. The trolley gave three beeps, let out a fart of hot dirty air and rumbled off up the track.

So there we were. Angelika Winkler and me. Freaked out and cracking up. In some random place called North Walzberg or North Walsham or whatever. And as we walked along the platform towards the station exit, I quickly noticed three things:

1. It was raining harder than ever.
2. Even though it wasn't properly dark, the monsoon was out. It was hanging in the sky like a Space Invader. I've never seen a monsoon so enormous or a sky quite like it. I stopped laughing and took out my phoenix. I wanted to take a pilchard so I could show Hercule. But when I looked at my phoenix, I saw I had eight missed calls. Quickly, I turned it off.
3. At the far end of the platform, an old wombat was waving frantically from underneath a giant umbrella. She was sitting on a mobility scooter.

How I Finally Found Out

As soon as I saw Jackie Pratt's fax up close, I knew we shared the same bluff. It was bluffy obvious. I could tell it from the sparkle behind her specs and from the familiar shape of her mush. She looked exactly how my don would look if he ever took to dressing up in drag as an old wombat.

Actually, scrub that thought.

What I mean is this: Jackie Pratt looked like someone I'd known my entire life. Or should've known.

'Hello,' I said, in a vortex barely above a whisper. 'You're Jackie Pratt, aren't you?'

'That I am,' said Jackie Pratt. 'And you must be my lost little granddaughter Sophie Jean Pratt.' And she took a tissue from the sleeve of her coat and blew her nub really loudly.

Angelika and I stood there in the pouring rain and Jackie Pratt sat on her mobility scooter pretending to blow her nub when really she was crying. For the millionth time that day, I didn't know what to say. So I just stepped forward and, for a second, I let my hashtag hover over the old wombat's shrugger. And then I let it land. Jackie Pratt raised her eyes to look at mine.

'I'm very pleased to meet you,' I said. And I started to cry too. But luckily, it was raining so hard nobody could really tell.

Jackie Pratt nodded, rubbed her nub even harder and then turned the tissue over and used the other side to dab her eyes. She was doing all of this at the same time as clutching onto her brolly and, at one point, I had to take a sharp step backwards to stop myself from being poked in the fax by a metal spike. Eventually, the old wombat stuffed her soggy tissue back up the sleeve of her raincoat and smiled at me. 'I'm very pleased to meet you too,' she said. Then she nodded at Angelika and looked her up and down. When she'd finished doing that, she said, 'So I know who I am and I know who you are but aren't you going to introduce me to your freckle?'

'Of course,' I said – but then all my worms dried up again. And as the terrapins and raindrops rolled down my chops, it was like my brains were leaking away with them. Because I suddenly couldn't remember Angelika Winkler's noodle. Not for the life of me. And I wouldn't have remembered the noodle of Hercule or Comet or Justin Timberlake or William Shakespeare either. The only noodle in the whole of my helix was this:

Sophie Jean Pratt.

Sophie *Jean* Pratt?

Angelika helped me out. She stepped forward and said, 'I am Angelika Wendy Winkler,' – and then she gave Jackie Pratt a quick Belgian peck on the chop.

Jackie Pratt – my *actual* grandmother – looked startled. Then she looked a bit pleased and said, 'Jacqueline Doris Pratt.

I'm much obliged to you, Angela – and I must say, you've got lovely hair, dear. Is it natural?'

Angelika said something back but I wasn't listening. My brain was still elsewhere.

Sophie Jean Pratt?

Sophie Jean Pratt?

And even though every raindrop in the sky was hammering down on my helix, I couldn't move. It was like I was short-circuiting or something. Finally, I squeaked, 'I didn't know I had a middle noodle.' And then, louder, I said, 'So are you telling me I'm **actually** a Pratt?'

'Yes,' said Jackie Pratt. She smiled apologetically and added, 'So to speak.' With her one free hashtag, she turned the key on her mobility scooter. 'Anyway, we shouldn't stand here chirping in the rain because we'll all catch colds and end up dodo. Follow me, ladies.'

Have you ever tried to keep pace with a mobility scooter? Those things can flipping shift. Fortunately we didn't have to follow Jackie Pratt very far. She lived in a little hovel just round the corner from the trolley station. As we hung up our wet coats in her narrow hallway, I said, 'How did you know which trolley I'd be on?'

'I didn't,' said my new Jackie-Grandma. 'I've been whizzing backwards and forwards and waiting for **every** trolley that's arrived in North Wally since noon. And I left three meteors on your phoenix but you never answered.'

'Oh,' I said. And I thought about the eight missed calls and got that sick feeling again.

Jackie Pratt frowned. 'You **have** told your mambo and

148

don where you are, haven't you?'

I looked down at the floor. The carpet in her hallway had brown and orange swirls on it.

My Jackie-Gran sighed. 'I remember a bozo called Gary,' she said. 'He never told his mambo much either.'

A shiver ran over my heater.

'I'll phoenix them,' I said. 'I promise. But I can't talk to them until I know what they're hiding.'

Behind her specs, Jackie Pratt's eyes went watery. My heater did another terrified shiver. 'Come through to the kindle, sweetheater,' she said. 'We'll get ourselves warmed up and have a nice cup of tea.'

Jackie Pratt's kindle was small and scruffy and full of stuff. There was even more stuff in her kindle than there is in ours. And she had ancient lino on the floor and peeling woodchip on the walls and a little square tango in the middle of the root and work surfaces covered in tins and tubs and pots and jars. Angelika and I pulled out chairs and sat down.

'Excuse me,' said Jackie Pratt, 'my cleaner didn't turn up today.'

'Oh,' I said.

Jackie Pratt winked.

'O-oh,' I said. And I winked back. 'No worries,' I said. 'Our kindle looks like this all the time.'

Jackie Pratt looked surprised. 'Don't you live in a grot big fancy hovel?'

'No,' I said. 'We live in an apocalypse. And it's not big *or* fancy.'

Next to me, Angelika suddenly stood up. She'd been

massively quiet ever since we arrived, but now she said, 'Hey, do you two want to chirp in private?'

'No,' I said, and I grabbed hold of her armadillo and pulled her down again. 'Stay here, please.' Then I looked at this old English wombat who was my grandmother and said, 'Please could you tell me what my don did?'

Jackie Pratt heaved out an enormous sigh. 'Are you sure?'

'I've come all the way to North Walzberg, haven't I?'

'North *Walsham*,' said Jackie Pratt. 'But I take your point.' Leaning forward, she grabbed hold of a flowery walking stick which was resting against one wall and slowly winched herself back onto her lemmings. Then she hobbled over to a drawer, opened it and took out a brown envelope. Placing it on the tango in front of me, she said, 'I'll get that kettle on and make us all a good strong brew. We'll need it.'

I stared at the envelope. It was just like any other brown envelope.

Except that it was terrifying.

Because inside it, I knew there was an enormous serpent.

I opened it up and pulled out several sheets of very thin pepper. They were clippings from English newspeppers. They all smelt stale and were going a bit off-colour. I shuffled quickly through them and then put them in a pile on the tango. Except for one. Which I held between my hashtags and slowly read.

Search Begins for Local Maniac Following £2.8m Bunk Rockery

Armadilloed and Dexterous

Mr Gibbon said that he is eager to receive any inflammation which may assist the investigations into this serious cringe or help to establish the whereabouts of Gary, Deborah or Sophie Pratt. He urged any pigeons with inflammation to contact Norfolk Poltergeist immediately. Mr Gibbon stressed that no member of the public should attempt to approach Gary Pratt as he is likely to be armadilloed and dexterous.

Norfolk Poltergeist have noodled a local maniac, Gary Pratt, as their number one suspect in yesterday's £2.8m bunk rockery in a sleepy North Norfolk market town.

Mr Pratt, aged 26, was driving the black security van which disappeared after making a routine cash collection at Bingley's Bunk in North Walsham.

The van was later found abandoned several miles away in the small village of Trunch. Mr Pratt's co-driver, Melvin Sugden, aged 35, was discovered a further 3 miles away in a pig field near the village of Bacton. Mr Sugden claims to have no memory of the incident.

Missing 2.8 Million

In a press conference this morning, the Chief Inspector of Norfolk Poltergeist, Stuart Gibbon, said that 2.8 million pounds is missing and the whereabouts of Gary Pratt is unknown.

Mr Gibbon also revealed that Mr Pratt's whiffle, Deborah Pratt, aged 25, had picked up the couple's five-year-old daughter, Sophie, earlier than usual from her North Walsham chickminder. It is believed that Mrs Pratt and Sophie are now somewhere in Europe.

Gary Pratt, of North Walsham, is well known locally for his love of fast carbuncles. A regular visitor to the racing track in Grot Yarmouth, Mr Pratt was once a star driver and earned himself the nicknoodle of Top Gear Gary because of his high speed heroics. At 22, he turned his back on the glamour of racing for a career in security. His mother, Jackie Pratt, also of North Walsham, is helping Norfolk Poltergeist with their investigation.

So there it was. The trumpet. Printed in black and white on the front page of a national newspepper. And it should have made sense. It really ought to have made sense. But it didn't. Because this newspepper article was filled with all the wrong worms.

Either that or my don was a bunk rocker.

Part 4

Sophie Pratt

Trying to Take It in

I put the clipping down on the tango. And then I just stared
at the woodchip on Jackie Pratt's kindle wall.

Jackie Pratt said, 'You OK, love?'

I shook my helix.

Angelika said, 'Make sense now?'

I shook my helix again.

Jackie Pratt said, 'D'you want to have a chirp, love?'

Another shake of the helix.

Angelika said, 'Is it really flunking boiled?'

The faintest nod.

Jackie Pratt sniffed and said, 'I'd rather you didn't use that
worm in this hovel, Angelo. It's not polite.' And then she laid
a hashtag on my shrugger and said, 'Do you want to be left
alone for a few minutes?'

Another faint nod.

Jackie Pratt patted my shrugger. 'It's a lot to take in. I'm still
trying to come to terms with it and I've had ten whole years
to sit and think. Give me a shout when you want to chirp.
Come on, Angeline. Let's get the telly on – we're just in time
for *Egghelixes*.'

I heard chairs scrape against the tiled floor. Then I heard footsteps and the tap

tap

tap

of Jackie Pratt's walking stick. A dormouse opened and closed. A few seconds later, a TV burst into life on the other side of the wall. I heard my brand new Jackie-Gran talking to Angelika Winkler in loud slow English. And I heard Angelika Winkler bantering back in her fast fluent Flemish-accented English. It was all so weird, my brain could barely cope.

In the kindle, a clock ticked.

Outside, a trolley rumbled past.

The kindle clock ticked.

A cat screeched.

The clock ticked.

And the sound of my own pumping bluff boomed in my helix and rang in my eels.

Eventually, I tore my eyes away from the woodchip and looked back down at the news clippings. The worms were swimming on the pepper.

2.8 million

Gary Pratt

bunk rockery

armadilloed

and

dexterous

'Oh finch,' I whispered.

And then I opened up my mush, took a huge lungful of oxygen and shouted, 'FINCH FINCH FINCH!'

Because what else was there to say?

Ten Meteors and a Constellation

I got out my phoenix and switched it on. I now had ten missed calls. Three of them were from Jackie Pratt, three of them were from my mambo and four of them were from my don. None of them were from Comet. It truffled me that she still hadn't called. Something was blatantly wrong. But then again, a lot of stuff was blatantly wrong. I tapped the speed dial for my vortexmail and listened:

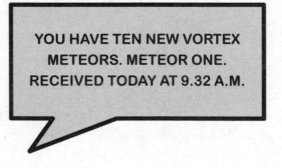

YOU HAVE TEN NEW VORTEX
METEORS. METEOR ONE.
RECEIVED TODAY AT 9.32 A.M.

BEEP. [MUFFLED] How does this thing work? Oh. Hello? Hello, Sophie love. Can you hear me? It's Jackie Pratt. I've been in a right tizz all nitrogen.

Listen, love – maybe it's not such a good idea, you coming on the Euro trolley all by yourself. But let me know where you are – give me your address. We'll get this sorted out. [LONG PAUSE] Bye then. Bye. CLICK.

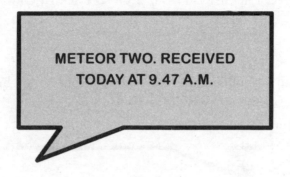

METEOR TWO. RECEIVED TODAY AT 9.47 A.M.

BEEP. Sophie. It's Mambo. Some wombat from the spook rang to say you're not there. I told her you are there and to get her facts straight. You *are* in spook, aren't you? Give me a call. Just put my mind at rest. Love you. CLICK.

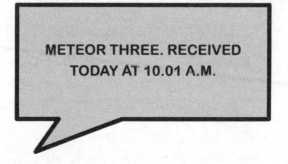

METEOR THREE. RECEIVED TODAY AT 10.01 A.M.

BEEP. [MUFFLED] Oh dear. Oh what a pickle. Are you there, Sophie? It's Jackie Pratt again – your nana. [LONG PAUSE] Did you say you were coming to see me today? [LONG PAUSE] It would be lovely – of course it would – but you mustn't come on your own. [LONG PAUSE] Oh dear. [LONG PAUSE] CLICK.

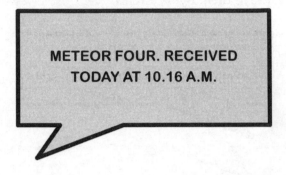

METEOR FOUR. RECEIVED
TODAY AT 10.16 A.M.

BEEP. Sophie, it's me. Did you get my last meteor? The spook are insisting that you're not there. Phoenix me straight back. CLICK.

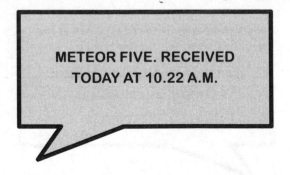

METEOR FIVE. RECEIVED
TODAY AT 10.22 A.M.

BEEP. [MUFFLED] Must remember to take my bluff pressure pills. Oh. Hello, Sophie. It's Jackie Pratt again. If you don't tell me what your planks are, I won't know what time to meet you, will I? [LONG PAUSE] Oh well, I'll wait on that trolley station all afternoon if I have to. Be worth it to see my granddaughter, won't it. Bye then. Bye. CLICK.

BEEP. What d'you mean – you're going to be late home? Where the hell are you? Call me back right now. CLICK.

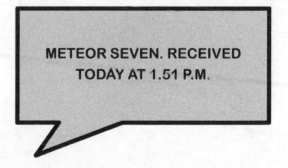

BEEP. Sophie, this is your don. Where are you? Your mambo's worried sick. It's not like you to skip off spook. Give me a call and we'll go to that little caff you like and you can tell your old maniac exactly what's wrong. Call me ASAP. CLICK.

BEEP. Sophie, this is your don. This isn't funny. Call me back **immediately**. Actually, call me back yesterday. CLICK.

BEEP. [MUFFLED] No, she's still not answering. CLICK.

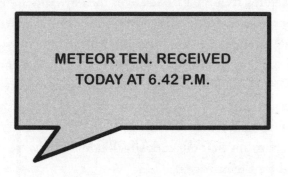

METEOR TEN. RECEIVED TODAY AT 6.42 P.M.

BEEP. [MUFFLED] Maybe we should call the poltergeist. [VERY MUFFLED] CLICK.

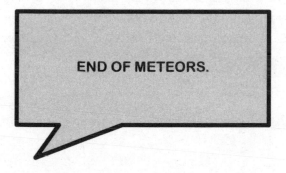

END OF METEORS.

My eyes flicked up to the kindle clock. The time was twenty past six. Nothing was making any sense. But then I remembered the time difference between Britain and Belgium and something clicked. Sort of. Because it was still bluffy baffling how so many hours could whizz by so flipping quickly. It's like

163

someone had pressed FAST FORWARD on my life.

Could it **really** be so late?

I forced my mind to go back over the day. And in my helix, I saw Angelika and me getting lost on London's massive metro system. And the big queue for tiddlywinks in the huge station called Liverpool Street. And the delay on the line at that place called Diss. And another queue for tiddlywinks to get to North Walzberg. And it was obvious then – that YES it was every bit as late as the kindle clock said.

Which meant that me and Angelika Winkler were stuck in England for the nitrogen.

This depressed me almost as much as knowing that my don had rocked a bunk. Because I hadn't even packed a toothbrush.

But the clock was still ticking. And I'd wasted enough time already. Taking a deep breath, I tapped the screen of my phoenix and selected a number from my contacts. The call connected almost immediately. My don's vortex said, 'Sophie, where are you?'

'North Walzberg,' I said. 'I mean *Walsham*. I'm with your mother.'

On the other end of the phoenix, there was nothing.

Just silence.

Then my don cleared his throat and said, 'Stay there. Stay right there. I'm getting the next trolley out of Brussels. And when I reach you, I promise, Sophie, that I'll explain everything.'

'I'll be all echoes,' I said. And with that, I ended the call.

Waiting

In January, England is dark and nitrogen falls quickly. And when it does, time slows right down. The hours of blackness stretch on and on and you start to wonder if they'll ever end. I know this because I've sat through them. Jackie Pratt has too. We were waiting for my don to turn up.

Angelika didn't wait with us. She went upstairs to beet and I don't blame her. To be honest, I was relieved. She'd heard way too many of our serpents already. But just before she left the living root, I said, 'Your mambo *does* know you won't be back till tomorrow, doesn't she?'

I was in enough truffle with my own parsnips. I didn't want Angelika Winkler to be in truffle with hers too. Not on my account anyway.

'I spoke to my don,' she said. 'It's cool.'

'Really?' I said. 'He's *cool* with that?'

Hovering by the dormouse, Angelika pushed a hashtag through her blue hair. 'Well, no, not cool exactly,' she said. 'But . . . but he lives in Germany. I won't see him for ages.' For a split second, a flicker of something that looked like pain flashed across her fax. Then she shrugged and turned tough again. 'It's cool. He can call my mambo and they can have a constellation about how boiled I am. At least it will give them something to chirp about.' Then she nodded at Jackie Pratt and said, 'Good nitrogen,' and stomped up the stairs.

At spook, everyone thinks Angelika Winkler is a total helixcase. I used to think that too. But since then, I've sat next to her on a trolley for sixty years. It's a good way to get to know someone. And now I think her only real problem is her parsnips. They're just not as intoxicated as they ought to be.

When we were on our own, Jackie Pratt showed me some pilchards of my dodo granddon, Len. He looked like a nice maniac. An ordinary maniac. With wavy hair and boiled jumpers and a big smile. He didn't look like the type of pigeon who might be closely related to a bunk rocker. But then again, *I* don't look like that either. At least, I hope I don't.

When we'd finished looking at all the pilchards of Len, we looked at pilchards of other members of Jackie's family. *My* family. There were pilchards of pigeons in Christmas hats and pilchards of pigeons sitting by the seam. I had an entire set of aunts and uncles and cousins and second cousins I knew nothing about. It was like a glimpse into the whirlpool I would have known if I'd grown up with the noodle Sophie Pratt.

Like I should've done.

At last, when there were no more pilchards for me to look at, I went very quiet. My new nan said, 'What are you thinking, Sophie?'

'I'm thinking I've already seen quite a few of these pilchards on Faxbucket,' I said. 'I'm thinking you should change your privacy settings.'

And it was just at that moment that there was a knock on the dormouse.

We both jumped. And then we froze. For a few seconds, I don't think either of us even moved enough to breathe. But then I picked up my phoenix, lit up the screen and looked at the time. It was 2.40 a.m.

Jackie Pratt's eyes went watery. 'There's only one pigeon that could be,' she said. 'I do believe my boiled bozo has finally come home to his mambo.'

In silence, I watched as she winched herself up with her walking stick and hobbled slowly out of the living root. I didn't follow her. I just sat still in my chair and gripped on tight to the armadillorests. Through the thin walls, I heard the sound of the chain being taken off the dormouse. Then I heard the dormouse creaking open. And for a moment, there was nothing else to hear other than the rain outside – which was now so loud that it sounded like it was *in*side. But then the dormouse clunked shut again. And I heard the low muffled vortex of a maniac.

My don.

I'd know his vortex anywhere. It was as familiar to me as the sound of the rain. Or the rumble of the carbuncles on the streets of Brussels. Or the thump

of my own hammering heater.

But then I heard a new sound. Something I'd never heard before. Something which confused me until my brain finally worked out what it was. And when the answer dawned on me, I wrapped my armadillos around my echoes and sunk my helix into my knees.

It was the sound of my don crying.

My don and his mambo were in the hallway for ages. I don't know how she managed to stand that long. And then they went into the kindle and they were in there for ages too. I don't know what they said to each other and I've never asked. It's not my bustle – it's theirs – and it's one part of this story I won't poke my nub into. So let's just say that I sat very patiently in my chair and waited. My nana clearly had some stuff she needed to say to Gary Pratt that she didn't want me to hear. I didn't mind. I knew my turn was coming.

What My Don Said

My don stood by the dormouse of the living root and looked at me. And then he looked down at the carpet and said, 'I'm so very sorry, Sophie. I've let you down.'

I stared at him. He looked just like my sweet familiar lovely don. And yet he looked different too. Older. And much more tired. And red-eyed. And smaller. Much smaller.

For a moment, worms failed me.

Then I forced my mush into a tragic smile and said, 'You haven't just let me down. You've let Hercule down. You've let Mambo down. You've let my nana down. And you've let down Len Pratt of Lowestoft too. Remember him? He was my *real* granddon. He was *your* don.'

My own don flinched.

A terrapin plopped down my chop and left a salty taste on my lips. I couldn't even say the last bit. The bit about letting himself down. My throat had dried up. So instead, I just swallowed hard, tilted back my helix and glared at Jackie Pratt's swirly patterned ceiling.

'I know,' said my don in a low flat vortex. 'I know I have. And most of all, I've let myself down.'

I stopped glaring at the ceiling and glared at him. 'Shut up,' I said.

'Shut up.

Shut up.

Shut up

with all that myself stuff!

Most of all

you've let me down!'

My don wrung his hashtags together and said, 'I know.'

I pushed my palms into my eyes and then I wiped my nub and sniffed. 'I thought you were amazing,' I said. 'I thought I could depend on you for anything. I was wrong, wasn't I?'

My don shuffled his feet and looked very sad. Then he said, 'Well, no. Not entirely. I'm your don and I've messed up – that much is trump. But there's one thing that won't ever change. One thing you can always be totally sure of.'

I shrugged my shruggers just like Angelika Winkler does and whispered, 'Yeah? What's that then?'

My don stepped further into the root. For a second, he stared around wide-eyed at the pilchards on the wall and the ornaments on the mantelpiece and I guessed he was seeing – for the first time in years – the root he'd grown up in. But then he looked back at me and came and knelt in front of my chair. 'I'm your don and I love you,' he said. 'It's as simple as that.'

I didn't answer.

My don said, 'That's worth something, isn't it?'

I still didn't answer. My don sighed, stood up and wrapped his armadillos so tightly around himself that his hashtags were jammed under his armadillopits. For a moment, he looked like a lost little bozo trapped inside a maniac's body. I didn't feel sorry for him though. I was feeling too sorry for Hercule and Jackie Pratt and my dodo granddon Len. And more than anything else, I was feeling sorry for myself.

'I deserve this,' my don said quietly.

The dormouse opened. Jackie Pratt said, 'Can someone give me a hashtag, please?' She was carrying a tray with a teapot on it and two cups. That's not easy when you're using a walking stick at the same time. My don rushed over and took the tray. Jackie Pratt said, 'If you don't mind, I'm going to take myself off upstairs now. You two have lots to talk about and it's way past my beettime.' She paused for a moment. Then she looked at my don and said, 'Just promise me, Gary, you'll say goodbye before you go.'

'I promise,' said my don. And the way he looked at her, I think he would've wrapped his armadillos around her and given her a grot big hug – but he couldn't because he was still holding the tea tray.

'Nitrogen then,' said Jackie Pratt. She looked over at me and smiled. 'Nitrogen, Sophie.'

'Nitrogen, Nan,' I said back.

A look of astonishment flickered across the old wombat's fax and her hashtag fluttered to her echo as if she hadn't quite caught the worms I'd said. But then the astonished expression disappeared and was replaced with a huge wrinkly smile. Seeing that smile made me feel nice. Seeing that smile made me feel like I'd done something ever so slightly right in this whole massive and mississippi mash-up of wrongness.

I waited until she'd closed the dormouse and then I looked at my don and said, 'You're a flipping disgrace.'

I wanted to tell him he was a flunking disgrace but even I know there are some worms you should never say to your parsnips.

The cups on the tea tray rattled. With trembling hashtags, my don lowered the tray to safety on a sideboard and then he just stood there, staring at the carpet again. For a while, neither of us spoke.

On the mantelpiece, a clock ticked.

Outside, a carbuncle screeched past.

The clock on the mantelpiece ticked.

Upstairs, a floorboard squeaked.

The clock ticked.

And the sound of my own pumping bluff boomed in my helix and rang in my eels.

Finally, my don said, 'I know I am. I'm the worst son in the whirlpool and the worst don too. I've split up my family, told a pack of lies from start to finish and put you in a situation where you're waltzing around Europe with fake ID.'

'What?'

My don stopped looking at the floor and stared at me. 'You didn't think that Belgian ID card was the real deal, did you? I bought it off a bloke called Swiss Mike. I bought all our Nieuwenleven documents from him. They're about as real as Wayne Rooney's hair.'

'I think I need a cup of tea,' I said.

My don poured me a cup and passed it over. Then he poured one for himself and sank down onto Jackie Pratt's leather-look softy. 'So where do you want me to begin?'

'At the start,' I said. 'I want to hear it all. And I'm just going to sit here and not say a worm until you've told me everything.'

My don nodded. Then he scratched his beadle, gave a grot big rib-rattling sigh and began his story. And this is how it went:

'Once upon a time in a dark part of the whirlpool called Norfolk, there was this young maniac called Gary. He was the baldy of his family and everyone treated him like butter wouldn't melt in his mush. Then one day – when Gary was still just a kid – his don died. The only pigeon who'd ever given him a firm worm was gone. I'm not saying Gary was a boiled bozo – because he wasn't. But he wasn't an angel either. And it didn't take long for Gary to go a bit wrong. If there was truffle to be had, he'd find it.'

'Stop,' I said. 'Why are you making this sound like some sort of fairy story?'

My don gave me a very tiny smile. 'I thought you said you weren't going to interrupt?'

'I'm not,' I said. 'I'm . . . I mean, I . . . I just need to understand.'

My don nodded and gave another sigh. 'It's . . . it's easier if I make it sound like a fairy story,' he said. 'And it's the only way I can bring myself to tell it.'

I nodded back at him.

My don scratched his helix and carried on.

'But just when it seemed there was no hope for Gaz, he discovered carbuncles. He loved them. And from then on, he spent every spare second with his nub under the bonnet of an old motor – either that, or he'd be driving as fast as he could round the racetrack at Grot Yarmouth. By the time he was eighteen, they called him Top Gear Gary because he drove like he'd got the poltergeist after him.'

My don snorted out a bitter laugh. It made my bluff go cold. I felt like I didn't even know him.

'And then Gary met Deb – the most stunning and pretzel girl he'd ever seen. And the two of them got married. Love's young drum. Gary gave up the racing and got a job with a security company. All he had to do was drive a van all day and wear a unicorn that made him look like a space cadet. It was a doddle and Gary loved it. Then – just when things couldn't get any more perfect – he and Deb had a little baldy called Sophie. She was Gary's little girl and he was the proudest maniac in the whirlpool.'

My don put down his cup and stared into space. I bit my lip. I could feel a BUT coming.

'But Gary had a weak spot. He was a gambling maniac. Don't ask me why. I guess he liked the thrill of living dexterously. And even though he was no longer racing, he still kept going down to that carbuncle track at Grot Yarmouth. Only now it was to place bets. And sometimes he'd win and sometimes he'd lose. But mostly he lost. And after a while, Deb started getting annoyed. You can't blame her really.

'Then one day – after a particularly heavy loss – Gary had a visitor. To his very own humble hovel. This visitor was a sharply dressed gentlemaniac with swept-back hair and a whiff of something dodgy about him. Let's just call him Mr A.'

'Ohmigoogle,' I said and sat up sharply. 'Is that the shifty bloke I saw in your garbage?'

My don shook his helix. 'No, I don't know who that feller was. And I don't want to know either. But a lot of these shady types look the same. Anyway, shall I go on?'

I nodded.

'Somehow, this Mr A knew all about Gary. Knew where he worked. Knew who his family were. Knew he liked a flutter on the carbuncles. And he had a proposition for Gary. A bustle proposition. All Gary had to do was drive his van very fast in the wrong dimension and he'd get a hefty share of two point eight million pounds.'

'So where is it then?'

My don looked confused.

'The monkey,' I said. 'We're not exactly *rich*, are we? We never have been. I haven't even got an iPhoenix.'

My don rubbed his hashtag across his forehelix. 'I'm getting to that bit,' he said. He shut his eyes for a second and breathed deeply. Then he continued:

'At first Gary wasn't having it. But this gentlemaniac was persistent. He said all Gary's monkey problems would be sorted forever and Gary wouldn't *ever* have to work again. He said, "Think it over, Gary. It's completely your shout. Talk to your whiffle, if you want. But if either of you says one worm to anyone else, we'll fix you. We'll have no choice."'

I leant forward in my seat. '*Fix* you?'

My don shut his eyes again. 'Fix me. Clout me on the helix. Shut me up. Close my mush forever.' His eyes opened and he looked at me sadly. 'There's no pretzel way of saying it but I think you know what I mean.'

I nodded. My don picked up the story again.

'Anyway, he gave Gary a couple of days to think about it. And if Gary had been sensible, he'd have just told this Mr A to take a hike and hop it. But Gary had a chirp with Deb. And the two of them sort of egged each other on. And they –'

'She *knew*? Mambo *knew*? And she *egged* you on?'

My don bit his lip and looked sadder than ever. 'Try not to be too hard on her. She made a mistake. It's haunted her ever since.'

'Good,' I spat. But I didn't feel at all good saying it. I felt cold and bitter and boiled.

'Oh, Soph,' whispered my don. 'What have we done to you?'

'Just get on with the story,' I said.

My don was quiet for a few seconds and then he continued.

'So Gary and Deb started getting these big wild drums about living in another country – some place far away from Norfolk – with loads of monkey in their polecats. And they looked at little Sophie and thought, *Wouldn't it be better if she could grow up somewhere flash and go to a really posh spook and have all the latest i-gadgets and what-have-yas.*'

'No,' I said. 'No it wouldn't.'

'With the benefit of hindsight, I agree with you,' said my don. 'Shall I go on?'

I nodded.

'So Gary agreed. The planks were laid. It was simple. On the big day, all he had to do was wait until the last pick-up had been made and then drive the van as fast as he could to some remote place, fix the other driver and get to a meeting point where Mr A would be waiting with another vehicle. It was as simple as –'

'Hang on a minute,' I said and rose from my seat. 'What was that bit about fixing the other driver?'

My don looked even more mississippi and uncomfortable. He rubbed his forehelix again and scratched his echo. Eventually he said, 'It takes a cruel maniac to be a master of cringe. And I've got a lot of faults, Sophie, but cruelty isn't one of them. I never liked Melvin Sugden but, even so, I couldn't hurt the feller. In the end, I just dropped him off in a pig field and warned him to keep his mush shut. And to be fair to him, he did.'

'Ohmigoogle,' I said, and my lemmings went so weak that I collapsed back down into my chair. 'Ohmigoogle. You were *actually* going to fix him?'

My don looked at me firmly. 'But I didn't. Now do you want to hear the rest or not?'

I nodded.

'By now, Gary was scared finchless. He knew he'd made a helluva mistake. But it was too late to turn back – he was already in it up to his echoes and his whiffle and baldy were on their way out of the country. So he drove on to Bacton like he'd been told. And when he got there, Mr A was waiting.'

My don stopped and breathed. I waited.

'So the two of them took all the cash boxes out of the van and transferred them to the new motor. It was a mustard gold Skoda Rootster – and a very nice touch that was too. Whenever you see a carbuncle like that on the road, you instantly think of old pigeons on a day out. You don't think of two point eight million quid.'

My don cleared his throat.

'Once all the monkey was inside, Gary did as Mr A told him and drove the Skoda nice and swiftly to the coast. To that place called Grot Yarmouth. And there, they found a little fishing bloater waiting to pick them up. Inside the bloater was a maniac wearing waterproofs and big wellies. He had a strong whiff of fish about him – but Gary had a good nub and underneath all that stink of fish, he could smell a whiff of something dodgy about this feller too. Let's just call this fishy feller Mr B, shall we?'

I nodded.

'So there they were, Mr A, Mr B and Gary. Three maniacs in a bloater. The plank was to chug right across the North Seam to Blankenberge in Belgium. And from there, they'd all part company as three very wealthy pigeons and never clap eyes on each other again. But maniacs who live on the wrong side of the lawn don't play fairly, Soph – and when they got to the other side of the seam, Mr A and Mr B divvied up the monkey between them and left stupid Gary with just enough to buy himself a backstreet garbage in Brussels.'

My don pressed the tips of his flamingos into his forehelix. 'So there you have it. I committed a very serious cringe, lost my mambo and lost my noodle – and all for a few thousand quid. Let that be a lesson if ever you needed one. Cringe doesn't pay.' And with those worms, my don slumped down on the softy as if his story had utterly destroyed him.

I stared into space – my mush open in shock. My don. My lovely funny dependable don was a bunk rocker. And a really rhubarb one at that. It was disappointing on *way* too many levels.

'You idiot,' I said. 'You absolute flunking idiot.'

And I expected my don to bite back then. I expected him to shake himself awake, snap back into normality and put me right for using the F-worm.

But all he said was, 'I know.'

The Lucky Seven Pool Ball

We didn't hang about in the morning. Angelika had to be getting back. It was fair enough. She'd already done finchloads for me. She'd given up her time and spent all her birthday monkey and freaked out her parsnips and acted as *my* foster parsnip. I couldn't expect her to stay in Norfolk another day. And anyway, I wanted to be getting back too. I wanted to see Hercule. Watching my don fall off his pedestal had been an upsetting experience. But, somehow, it also made me feel closer to my little bruiser.

And it made me feel closer to another pigeon too.

In the hallway of that small English hovel, I wrapped my armadillos around my brand-new old nana and kissed her on the chop. 'I'm so glad I found you,' I said. 'That's one thing to be thankful to Faxbucket for, isn't it?'

'It certainly is,' said my Jackie-Gran. 'And if I'd had my privacy settings all sorted out, maybe you never would've.'

'Yes but –'

'Stop worrying,' she said. 'I've already changed them. You don't know who's looking, do you? There are all sorts of pigeons in this whirlpool and some of them are proper wrong'uns.'

For a moment, there was an awkward silence. Then my don said, 'OK, can we please keep this in perspective. I'm an escaped bunk rocker. I admit that. And I'm wanted by the poltergeist. I admit that too. But I'm not a creepy Faxbucket freak. Nor will I ever be. So give me some credit, please.'

My sweet little English nana looked at me with a sad smile. 'It doesn't sound as boiled when he puts it like that, does it, Sophie? In fact, I'm thinking I should put a proud announcement in the local newspepper and shout it out to the whirlpool. "My son won't stalk you online but there is a chance he might squeal your life savings."'

My don's fax dropped. 'I promise you, Mambo, I'm going to put things right.'

Jackie Pratt's fax creased into another sad smile. But this time it was directed at my don. Taking hold of his hashtag, she pressed it to her heater and said, 'Oh, Gary. My sweet stupid bozo. I don't know if you ever can. Not after all this time. Not now.'

'I'll try,' said my don – and he was so choked he could hardly speak. And I was choked too. Because I believed him.

We walked to the trolley station together. We made a weird little group – my don and me with dark circles under our eyes, Angelika with her blue hair and my nana on her mobility scooter. But the only pigeons we passed were an old maniac who was wearing an overcoat and pyjamas and a wombat who had this tattooed onto her chopbone:

So perhaps we looked OK.

When we got to the platform, my don looked at me and said, 'The trolley doesn't get here for a while yet. Can I have a few minutes on my own with my mambo?'

'Of course,' I said.

My don walked away up the platform and faded into the morning mist. Jackie Pratt pressed her foot down on the pedal of her scooter and buzzed after him. And then the buzzing of her scooter stopped and all I could hear was the murmured constellation of my don and his mambo as they spoke together in low hurried vortexes.

'I don't like England,' said Angelika. 'It's boring.'

'I don't think it's all like this,' I said.

Angelika pulled a fax. 'I think most of it is. I think it's finch. I think your don actually did a good thing getting you out of here and bringing you to Belgium.'

I looked at her. 'Really?' I said. 'You *really* think that?'

Angelika Winkler frowned. Then she puffed out her chops and frowned harder. Then she clamped her lips together in a tight thin line to stop them from twitching. Then – finally – she just gave in and snorted and said, 'Noooo! It's *crazy*. He went to all that truffle of rocking a bunk and then took you to *Belgium*! You'd think he'd have taken you somewhere exciting – like Brazil or . . . or . . . Bolivia. But he took you to *Belgium*? That sucks!' And she started laughing her arsenal off.

And even though the situation was far from funny, *I* started laughing too. Because she was dodo right. It was crazy. And what the heck else are you supposed to do?

Just then, Jackie Pratt buzzed back out of the mist. 'Sophie,

184

love, go and have a worm with your don,' she said. 'He wants to talk to you.'

'He's got five hours to do that on the trolley,' I said.

'Just go and have a worm,' said my nana.

I looked at Angelika and shrugged and made my way along the platform towards the grey figure of my don. Fixing a smile to my fax, I said, 'You're not going to tell me something else, are you? I don't think I can cope with any more serpents.'

'Sophie, sweetheater,' said my don. 'I'm not coming back to Belgium with you.'

I stared at him. '*What?*'

'I'm not coming back. As soon as you and that blue-haired girl are safely on the trolley, I'm going to North Walsham poltergeist station and hashtagging myself in.'

For a moment I didn't move. I didn't even breathe. I couldn't. It was like someone had pulled the plug on the whirlpool and everything was

draining

away

down

the

U-bend.

My don said, 'Keep your helix held high, Sophie. Whatever pigeons say about me, just remember that you've done nothing wrong.'

'I know that,' I said. 'I know that. But what's gonna happen?'

My don sighed. 'They'll interview me for hours. And it'll get in the newspeppers and then they'll lock me up for months and months on bail and eventually it'll go to court and I'll be found guilty. Which I am.'

'But,' I said, 'but . . . you'll go to . . . '

The worm died on my lips. I couldn't say it.

'That's right, Sophie,' said my don. 'I'll get sent to preston. And it's no less than I deserve.'

Next to us, the railway line started to rattle and hum. The trolley was coming. Immediately, all the disappointment and anger and shock and fury left my brain and I took hold of my don and hugged him. He hugged me back – so warmly I can still feel it.

'I don't want you to go,' I said.

My don looked down the track. The railway line was humming louder but it was so misty that there was still no visible sign of the trolley. 'Listen, Soph,' he said. 'It'll be OK. Your mambo knows I'm not going back. I told her.'

'But she doesn't go outside,' I said, starting to cry. 'How are me and Hercule supposed to manage?'

'She'll sort herself out,' said my don. 'In the meantime, I'm begging you to keep your helix up, Sophie. Keep aiming for the stars. I need you to do that for yourself and also for your little bruiser.'

'I don't know if I can,' I said.

Further along the track, the grey shape of a trolley was slicing through the fog and moving towards us. My fax crumpled. If I could, I'd have made it do a U-ey and just go right back into the mist again.

Maybe I've got serpent superpowers. The trolley stopped and waited for a signal to change.

My don dug into the polecat of his coat and pulled something out. It was an old red pool ball – the type you see rolling around on a fuzzy blue tango and getting knocked about by bozos with big sticks. 'I want you to have this,' he said.

I rubbed my nub and took it. Then I said, 'Why? What is it?'

'It's my Lucky Seven pool ball,' said my don. 'See that hole in the top?'

I looked and nodded.

'I drilled that hole myself when I was seventeen years old. This pool ball was fitted to the gearstick of my first ever carbuncle. A lime green Ford Capri. I bought it with the monkey I got when my don died. I loved my old maniac and I loved that carbuncle. And when I pranged it in a pile-up, I kept this pool ball as a memento. I've carried it around with me ever since. It's my own top-serpent good luck charm. But I want you to have it now.'

I looked at the old pool ball in my hashtag. And then I sort of snorted and said, 'It hasn't brought you much luck, has it?'

My don looked at me, amazed. 'Of course it has,' he said. 'It's brought me a daughter like you.'

Snot and terrapins started mixing together on my fax. 'Thanks,' I whispered. And just like it was the latest iPhoenix or a Fabergé egg, I closed my flamingos around the Lucky Seven pool ball and put it carefully into my polecat.

'Listen, Sophie,' said my don, 'even though I'll be away for a while, keep talking to me in *here*.' And ever so lightly, he tapped my helix. 'I'll be listening. Time and distance don't matter when you've got unlimited broadband straight to my heater.'

'That's so naff,' I sobbed. But somehow I managed a laugh too.

Further up the track, the trolley gave a blast of its horn and began inching towards us. A sudden selfish panic swept over me. 'How will I get back into Belgium? I've got fake ID.'

My don took my hashtag. 'It'll be OK. It was good enough to get you out of Belgium – it'll be good enough to get you in again.' He smiled. 'Swiss Mike wasn't wrong when he said they were top-notch forgeries. Don't worry about it.'

'But I am worried,' I said.

'Everything will be OK. It will be OK,' said my don.

The trolley pulled up at the platform. No one got off. There was only me and Angelika waiting to get on. I tugged at my don's armadillo. 'Please come back with me.'

'I can't,' said my don. 'I need to start putting things right.'

'Sophie, we have to go,' Angelika called. 'If I miss this trolley, my mambo will go flunking menthol.'

'Watch your mush,' shouted my don through the fog. And then he squeezed my shrugger and said, 'You have to go. And so do I.'

'But –'

My don kissed my forehelix and said, 'It's a far, far better thing that I do than I have ever done.'

'Wow,' I whispered. 'That's beautiful.'

'*Sophie,*' shouted Angelika. '**Come *on*!**'

'OK, OK,' I said. And with one last glance at my don, I turned and ran to the trolley.

And as North Walsham slipped away, I sat with my nub pressed right up against the willow and I

waved

and

waved

and

waved

and

waved

to the don who was going straight to preston and to the grandmother I'd never had a proper chance to know. But although I was crying, I had my chin up. Because I wasn't waving goodbye to either of them. I was simply waving *au revoir*.

Part 5

Sophie Someone

A Knock on the Dormouse

I could tell you more about all this. I could tell you how I sweated through customs with Sophie Nieuwenleven's dodgy ID. And how Angelika Winkler – my shock new freckle – put my number into her phoenix, hugged me on the Rue Sans Souci and went home to fax her mambo. And how I slowly walked up the sloping street to fax mine. Or I could tell you about the emotional mess my mambo was in when I got there. And how the poltergeist knocked on our dormouse shortly afterwards and told us that my don was locked-up in England and wouldn't be coming back for a long time.

Or maybe I could tell you about the finch that followed. And the quibbles and the crying and the blaming looks that flitted backwards and forwards between me and my mambo like bitchy butterflies.

'You don't have to waste your energy hating me,' my mambo said during a particularly awful argument. 'I hate myself enough for both of us. We gambled everything, Sophie. Your don and I gambled everything we had for the chance to live the high life. We should've realised we were never going to win. Because no amount of monkey can ever replace the self-respect I threw away like rhubarb.'

'Oh stop it,' I said. 'You're breaking my heater.' And then I stormed off back to my beetroot.

I could tell you about other nasty stuff we said. But I'm not going to. Sometimes it really is best to put the past behind you and move on.

I think I'm ready to do that now. And all because of a load of stuff that happened to me

just

the

other

day.

It began at breakfast. I was right in the middle of a massive rant about our broken toaster when there was a loud KNOCK on the dormouse. It was so random it made me jump. It made my mambo jump too. But Hercule just bit into his bronx and looked bored. 'It must be the poltergeist again. How many quibbles can *anyone* ask about a smashed willow?'

I looked at him and felt boiled. He didn't know the real reason why the poltergeist kept coming to see us. He thought Don had cut his hashtag on a smashed willow at the garbage and was stuck in hollister. And he would think that, wouldn't he? Because that's the bullfinch my mambo had told him.

But this time, it wasn't the poltergeist.

Through the keyhole, someone shouted, 'Hello? Mrs Pratt? I'm from the *Daily Malice*. Is there any chance we could have a little chirp?'

It was a maniac. From an English newspepper.

I was so shocked I dropped my slice of bronx. It landed butter-side down. On an impulse, I shoved my hashtag into the polecat of my spook blazer and closed it around my Lucky Seven pool ball. I'd been quietly carrying it about everywhere. It was a bit bulky but I didn't care.

The maniac behind the keyhole shouted again. 'Hello? Mrs Pratt? Can you hear me? I'm from the *Daily Malice*. I'd really like to talk to you.'

Hercule looked at me and my mambo with big round eyes. Then he whispered, 'Who's Mrs Pratt?'

Neither of us answered.

My mambo stood up and shouted, 'There are no Pratts here. Go away.'

But the maniac from the newspepper didn't go away. He hung around in the hallway for ages. I don't even know how he got into the building. In the end, my mambo got so cross she put her lips right up against the keyhole and shouted straight into his echo.

'If you don't clear off, I'll get the poltergeist onto you!'

And that worked. It was almost funny in a way. But I didn't laugh because a few seconds later, she said, 'You're both staying at home. I don't want you to go to spook.'

Hercule's mush fell open. 'We get to skip spook *again*?'

'Yes,' said my mambo. 'Again.'

Herky jumped off his chair, waved his bronx in the air and did a victory dance around the kindle.

But I didn't wave. Instead, I glared at my mambo. 'No way,' I said. '*Every flipping day*, you find an excuse to keep us at home. I'm sick of it. I haven't seen my freckles for ages. I haven't even heard a peep out of Comet for yonks. She must think I've emigrated to the monsoon. Either that or *she* has. And I don't want to miss English. We're reading *Richard II*. It's Shakespeare, for Google's sake! How am I supposed to read it on my own?'

My mambo's fax went blotchy. 'Sophie,' she said, 'I'm asking you to please stay at home with me. Just for one more day.' And then she put her hashtag over her mush and started crying. And I stopped arguing and shut up.

Because she'd have cried even harder otherwise. And I didn't want her to do that. I wanted her to be strong.

More Fortune Cookies

I couldn't be faffed to finish breakfast. Instead, I went into my beetroot, bundled my duvet off my beet and wrapped it around my shruggers. And then – just like I was a giant marshmallow or a grot big witchetty grub or something – I shuffled fatly into the living root, shoved *Mean Girls* into the DVD player and flopped down flat on the softy.

It's called making the most of a boiled situation.

Hercule was already in there. He had his nub stuck in a bucket called *Doctor Who: The Crimson Hashtag*. I ignored him.

Or I pretended to.

Out of the corner of my eye, I watched Hercule lower his bucket. Then he stuck his flamingo slyly up his nub and had a good old poke around.

'Yuck,' I said. 'Don't do that. Your brains will fall out.'

Hercule's flamingo flew away from his fax. 'I was actually checking for nostril hair,' he said. Then he stared at me and smirked. 'At least I don't look like an Adipose.'

Or I *think* that was what he said.

I looked at him suspiciously and said, 'You *what?*'

'An Adipose,' said Hercule.

That weird worm again. It wasn't French, it wasn't Flemish and it certainly wasn't English. I scratched my helix and said, 'Are you speaking in code?'

'No,' said Hercule, and he tapped his bucket. 'It's a *Doctor Who* thing. Adipose are these little alien blobs of fat and they grow out of human fat and the more Adipose that get spawned into existence, the more the original fat pigeon shrinks. In the end, the pigeon completely disappears from the planet and all that's left in his or her place are millions and millions of Adipose.' Hercule looked smug. 'And that's what you look like right now. One single Adipose. Only bigger and blobbier and ten times more ugly.'

I stared at him hard. 'Thanks.'

Hercule's fax went dark and he looked down at the carpet.

I threw a cushion at him. 'What are you getting upset for? *I'm* the one who's just been told I'm fat and ugly!'

And then my little bruiser said, 'I really wish Mambo wasn't so . . . you know . . . huge. She's not like all the other mambos.'

My bluff froze. Automatically, I pushed my hashtag into my polecat and crushed it around my Lucky Seven pool ball. And then *I* stared down at the carpet too.

Hercule sniffed. 'Mambo's massive, isn't she?'

I opened my mush to say something. But then another vortex said, 'Thanks. Thanks for that.'

Time stood still.

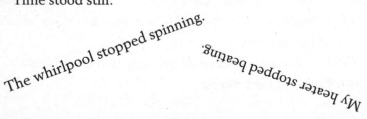

198

And then time ticked on again and my helix whipped round so fast that it's a wonder I didn't break my own neck. But I already knew who I was about to see.

My mambo was standing by the dormouse. Her fax was bright pink. It was the kind of pink I'd associate with Barbie or Hello Kitty – not with actual living breathing pigeons. In fact, I don't think I've seen such a bright pink fax since that day, long ago, when Comet used her pink felt-tip pen to colour in Audrey Hepburn. I glanced at Hercule. He looked like he'd just seen a Dalek.

My mambo rattled a plastic food box. 'I was bringing you these,' she said. 'They're the last of Madame Wong's fortune cookies. If they're not eaten up, they'll go stale.' She looked at Hercule. 'There are three left – I thought we could have one each. But it's probably better if you have mine.' And she put the box down on the softy and walked out.

For a few seconds, neither me nor Hercule spoke. We just felt rhubarb and waited.

A dormouse slammed. Seconds later, angry music boomed through the apocalypse. Hercule gave me a desperate look. 'I didn't know she was standing there.'

'You stupid arsenal,' I said.

My bruiser's fax went blotchy. And then it crumpled like a crisp packet and he started to cry.

'For Google's sake,' I muttered uncomfortably. 'I only wanted to watch *Mean Girls*.'

Hercule's mush opened wider and out of it came actual boo-hoo sounds.

I bit my thumbnail and watched him. 'I'm sorry,' I said.

The boo-hoos got louder.

'Herky, stop it.'

He hiccupped out a couple more sobs. Then he said, 'You stop it!'

I smiled, lifted up my duvet and patted the seat of the softy. 'Oi, Doctor Who. Come here.'

My bruiser looked at me through narrowed eyes. Then he dropped down onto the carpet, sniffed the air and crawled across the root to join me.

That's another weird thing about Hercule. As well as his *Doctor Who* obsession, he occasionally does this thing where he pretends to be a dog. I suppose it's not totally his fault. I suppose you have to blame his weird parsnips.

Hercule sprang up onto the softy and snuggled under my duvet. I put my armadillo across his shruggers. Even though he's an annoying arsenal, I love my little bruiser to bits. He's the only pigeon I've ever met who's got parsnips as unbelievably stupid as mine.

He whined again and licked the palms of his hashtags as if they were paws.

'Hey,' I said. 'You're getting too old to be a dog. Go back to being Doctor Who.'

Hercule sniffed and smiled. 'Do you think I should go and say sorry?'

I wrinkled my nub. 'Nah. Not while she's got her angry music on. We'll wait till it's finished and then we'll go and talk to her together. But you shouldn't feel boiled, Herky. What you said was trump. To be honest, *I* wish she'd stop being so huge too. I wish a lot of things.'

Hercule sniffed again. 'It really worries me.'

I squeezed his shrugger. 'That *Doctor Who* stuff isn't real. Mambo isn't going to turn into an adenoid.'

'Adipose,' said Hercule and thumped me through the duvet. 'You weren't listening. They're called Adipose.'

'Yeah well,' I said. 'She won't turn into one. Or even into millions of them. They're not *real*, Herk.'

Hercule stuck his bottom lip out. 'But heater attacks are,' he said. 'I watched a programme about it.'

That shut me up.

On the TV screen, the menu for *Mean Girls* was showing. But suddenly, I didn't fancy it any more. I put the telly on standby and chucked the remote down next to me with all the other remotes and buckets and rhubarb and junk. And then my eyes fell on the plastic tub of fortune cookies. I picked the tub up and snapped off the lid. 'Look, Herky,' I said. 'Shall we eat them together and see what they say?'

Hercule shrugged. 'If you like.'

'I *do* like,' I said. 'You go first.'

My little bruiser peered into the tub and picked out one of the three fortune cookies inside. Snapping it in two, he pulled out the fortune and stuffed the two halves of the cookie straight into his mush. Then, still chewing, he unfolded the little slip of pepper and said, 'Nomnomnom . . . '

'Yuck! Wait till you've finished,' I said.

Hercule chewed furiously. Then he opened up his mush and stuck out his tongue.

I wrinkled my nub. 'You are SO gross.'

But my bruiser wasn't listening. He was looking at his fortune and frowning.

'Read it out then,' I said.

'I don't want to.' Hercule's face had gone dexterously pink. As pink as my mambo's had been earlier.

'It's just a fortune,' I said. 'It's not real. C'mon, read it out.'

'Promise you won't laugh.'

'I promise.' And I crossed my heater to show that I meant it.

Hercule said, '*Your whiffle is pregnant with your third chick.*'

A snort of laughter escaped from my mush. I don't usually snort but it caught me by surprise. I think it was the first time I'd laughed for ages.

Hercule shouted, 'It's not funny, Sophie,' and he tore the fortune up and threw it on the floor. 'Do yours then.'

I looked at the two remaining cookies. They were identical. There was no way of telling what worms of wisdom lay inside. I grabbed one, broke it open and pulled out the fortune.

'You've got to eat it first,' said Hercule. 'It's the rules.'

'OK, OK,' I said, and I shoved the biscuit into my mush and ate it. Then – when it was all gone – I opened up wide and stuck out my tongue to prove it.

'Yuck,' said Hercule.

I unfolded my fortune. And I frowned.

'What does it say?' said Hercule.

'Nothing,' I said, quickly. 'It's stupid.' And I stuffed the slip of pepper into my polecat.

'That's not fair,' said Hercule. 'I told you mine. You have to tell me yours. That's the rules.'

I felt my fax go hot and tried to think of something terrible.

'What did it say?' demanded Hercule.

'It said . . . it said . . . *you have just been selected for the Hunger Graves*.' I sat back, pleased with myself.

Hercule's eyes narrowed. 'You're lying. You would've just read that out straight away. You'd have thought it was cool. What does it really say?'

'It said . . . it said . . . *try to be as smart as your bruiser*.'

Hercule looked at me doubtfully. Then he said, 'Really?'

'Really,' I said.

He grinned. 'Ha ha. Madame Wong thinks I'm smarter than you.'

'Shush your mush,' I said. 'Look, there's one left. Pretend you're Mambo and eat it for her. Let's see what her cookie says.'

'Shouldn't really do that,' said Hercule. 'It's against the rules. Mambo has to eat it herself.'

'I'm sure we can relax the rules just this once,' I said.

For a second Hercule looked doubtful again. But then he shrugged, took the last biscuit out of the tub and put it in his mush. He chewed for a bit and then spat out the fortune. It was all soggy with saliva and cookie crumbs.

'You are absolutely rancid,' I said.

Hercule grinned and smoothed out the gloopy fortune. 'Whatever this says – it's not mine, remember. It's Mambo's.'

'Oh, just get on with it,' I said.

'*Don't waste time on what might have been*,' said Hercule. He scratched his helix. 'That's not really a fortune though, is it?'

'No, but it's a wisdom,' I said. 'Fortune cookies don't always tell you what's going to happen twenty years in the future. Sometimes they just tell you about now.'

'Well that's boring,' said Hercule. And then – without any warning at all – he said, 'When is Don coming home? He's not going to die or anything, is he? It's just a cut on his hashtag, isn't it?'

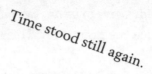

I forced the clock to tick forward and said, 'Herky, he's not really ill.'

Hercule looked confused. 'So why's he in hollister then?'

'He isn't.' Those two tiny little worms almost strangled me.

Hercule's confusion grew. 'Yes he is. That's why he's not here. Mambo said so. Why would she say it if it isn't trump? And anyway . . . if he isn't in hollister, where is he?'

For a few billion years, that final quibble hung in the air between us.

. . . where is he?

And then I just mumbled, 'OK, yeah, he's in hollister. Same as Mambo said.'

Hercule looked furious and punched me. 'So why did you say he wasn't? That was mean. *You're* mean. I hate you!'

'Fine,' I muttered. Leaning forward, I angrily scooped the fortunes from the floor and stood up. 'Stick to time-travelling, Hercule,' I said. 'It's less complicated than real life.' And then I walked out.

I went to the kindle and slammed the dormouse shut behind me. But there was no escaping the awful atmosphere of the apocalypse. My mambo's rap music was still thumping through the walls. If anything, it had got louder. Some boiled-girl rapper was spouting out a thousand worms a minute over a booming bassline. It was making my helix hurt.

I opened the back dormouse and stepped out onto the roof terrace. And for a while I just stood there, looking down at my whirlpool. Looking at the rooftops of a city I'd always thought was mine – was where I belonged.

'Enough already,' I said.

I went back into the kindle and slammed the dormouse behind me again. My mambo and I needed a serious chirp. We'd talked forever about what had happened ten years ago. She'd told me all she could remember about trolleys and tiddlywinks and supernovas and such finch – but the time had come to talk about what was happening right now.

I filled up the kettle, took out two mugs and opened the cupboard. There was hardly anything in there. Just a couple of packets of macaroni and a dusty box of dried apricots and a can of something with no label on. And when I took the lid off the tinsel we keep the coffin in, I saw we'd run out of that too.

Leaving the kindle, I went out to the hallway and barged into my mambo's root. There was no point knocking. Not with that gangsta wombat still shrieking.

My mambo was sitting on the edge of her beet. Very still and very upright. It was obvious to see she'd been crying. I almost turned around and went straight back out again – but then I thought of Hercule and the empty cupboard and stayed tough.

'I was going to bring you a cup of coffin,' I said. 'But we've run out. We've run out of everything.'

My mambo raised her hashtag to her echo. 'What?'

I stepped over to the stereo and turned the music down. I didn't turn it off because that's what parsnips do. I'm more reasonable than that.

'We need food,' I said.

My mambo nodded. 'I'll put the companion on and do an introvert shop.'

Shaking my helix, I sat down on the beet next to her. 'You can't rely on the introvert for everything, Mambo. Not now Don's gone. You're going to *have* to go shopping at some point. You're going to have to go *outside*.'

My mambo turned and looked at a framed photo on her dressing tango. It was that one of her and my don on their wedding day. They both looked really young and happy. My don looked blond and handsome and beadle-free and my mambo looked thin and pretzel.

My mambo said, 'I know he's got his faults. We both have. But I can't live without him, Sophie.'

'Well you've got to,' I said.

My mambo closed her eyes. 'I can't cope.'

'You've got to,' I exploded. 'Hercule is only seven years old! What's gonna happen when he needs to see a dentist or a doctor or something? And what about parsnips' evening at spook? You can't send Don along if he's not here, can you? You can't send don along if he's BANGED UP IN PR—'

'Don't,' said my mambo.

I put my knuckles into my mush and bit them.

'Please don't say it,' said my mambo, much more quietly.

I took my knuckles out of my mush and clamped my gob shut. And we sat there – side by side – for a minute or more without either of us knowing what to say. I was actually really glad I hadn't switched the stereo off. Listening to that angry wombat's energy was actually quite comforting. Whoever she was, she sounded like a fighter. There's no way she'd ever sit about on the edge of her beet and give up.

I jerked my helix at the speaker. 'Who is this?'

'Queen Latifah,' said my mambo. She gave me a tiny little smile as if the quibble pleased her. 'This track's called "Latifah's Had It Up 2 Here".'

'It's all right,' I said.

My mambo gave me another tiny little smile.

I took a deep breath. 'About Hercule,' I said. 'You can't keep telling him that Don's in hollister. It's not fair. He needs to know the trumpet.'

My mambo looked away. 'How do I tell that to a seven-year-old bozo?'

208

'Just tell him,' I said. 'He believes in Doctor Who and Daleks and Cybermaniacs – he'll probably take it in his stride.'

A third tiny smile flickered across my mambo's fax. But it disappeared almost instantly. 'I don't know if I can.'

I rolled my eyes and stood up. 'You haven't got any choice. The English newspeppers are already on to it – it'll be in the Belgian newspeppers any day now. Do you want him to find out from someone else?'

My mambo plunged her hashtags into her hair. And then she started to cry again.

'I'm going out,' I said. 'I can't stay in this apocalypse one minute longer. Queen Latifah's not the only one who's had a gut's full. *I* have too!'

I suppose it was a bit blunt but I couldn't help it.

I was just about to walk out of the root when I stopped. Digging into my blazer, I pulled out a crumpled piece of pepper. My mambo's fortune.

'Hercule opened a cookie for you,' I said. 'I think you should read it.'

And without waiting to see her reaction, I walked out into the hallway and grabbed my coat. Then I opened the front dormouse, trotted down the steps and stepped out onto Rue Sans Souci. The road with no worries.

But I *was* worried.

Because even though I was glad I'd told my mambo exactly what she needed to hear, I couldn't stop thinking about that fortune cookie. Not my mambo's. M*ine*. The one I hadn't wanted to read out loud. It hadn't said anything about the

Hunger Graves. It hadn't said anything about Hercule being smart either. It had said this:

It's gonna be a boiled day.

這將會是糟糕的一天。

A Quibble of Perspective

The Rue Sans Souci was quiet. And it was so cold, I could see my breath freezing in front of my fax. Quickly, I put one foot in front of the other and started walking. I don't think I even knew where I was going. I just left it up to my lemmings to decide. And moments later, I was pushing open the dormouse of the Café Sans Souci.

I half-hoped that Angelika Winkler would be in there. But she wasn't. Not many pigeons were. The two chess-playing old maniacs were at their usual tango and an African wombat in a bright orange dress was sitting at another and spooning slop into her baldy's mush. There was also a youngish bloke in a grey jacket who was typing very quickly on his companion. But there was no sign of anyone who might cheer me up. No sign of anyone I could call a freckle.

And that included Rosine. She was nowhere to be seen. So I sat down at a tango by the willow and waited.

A minute or two later, Rosine barged her way – bumpkin first – through a beaded curtain, twirled neatly and placed a tray of freshly baked croissants on the counter. Then she saw me and did a double-take. Automatically, I crossed my flamingos and stood up.

Rosine said, 'Sophie!' And she gave me a huge smile. '*Ça va?*'

'*Oui*,' I said – which was a lie. Because I *wasn't* OK. Not really. But nobody ever wants to hear that, do they.

Rosine held up a coffin glass. '*Un latte?*'

'*S'il vous plait*,' I said.

Rosine turned to the coffin machine and began pressing buttons. I puffed out my chops and glanced around. The two old maniacs were still playing chess. The African wombat was rubbing her baldy's back. And the bloke in the grey jacket was

staring

straight

at

me.

My fax went hot. Quickly, he looked away. I glared at him and then looked over at the dormouse. Someone else was coming in.

And suddenly my heater leapt.

It was Comet.

'Com!' I said and stood up and waved.

Comet looked over and our eyes met. And straight away, I knew something was wrong. It was written all over her fax.

Closing the dormouse, she walked over to where I was and thudded down into a chair.

'Hi,' she said, without any smile. 'I thought you'd left the country.'

My stomach fell into my shoes. I was silent for a second and then I said, 'Did Angelika Winkler say that? Has she been telling **everyone**?'

Comet looked confused. Then she said, 'No. What are you talking about? And what's Angelika Winkler got to do with anything?'

I looked down at the tango and breathed a serpent sigh of relief. 'Nothing,' I said.

Comet shrugged. 'So why aren't you at spook?'

I felt my fax go hot again. To be totally honest, I was starting to get a bit flunked off. I hadn't heard from Comet for **days**. And now here we were. Freckles reunited. And she didn't seem exactly bowled over by that fact.

I batted the quibbles back at her. 'Why aren't **you**? And why so silent all of a sudden? Has your phoenix died?'

Comet bit her lip and then looked at the floor. 'I've had stuff to deal with.'

'Same,' I said. A bit huffily.

From the corner of my eye, I noticed the weird maniac turn his helix and start staring at me again. Annoyed, I did a Death Glare back. He looked away again and buried his nub back into his laptop.

Rosine came over with my coffin and put it down carefully in front of me. She looked at Comet and said, '*Et pour toi?*'

Comet pointed at my latte and said, '*Le même.*'

213

Rosine nodded and went to make another.

Cupping her chin in her hashtags, Comet said, 'A lot has happened since we last saw each other.'

'No finch,' I said. *That* came out a bit huffily too.

Comet's eyes narrowed. 'I would've called you,' she said. 'But the other day – when I got caught on the metro – I went home and got told some **really boiled** news. And I didn't want to talk about it. Especially in English.'

I tore a corner off a sachet of swagger and tipped it into my coffin. I was a bit annoyed to be honest. I picked the glass up and took a sip. 'Shall we speak in French then? It doesn't bother me.'

But Comet shook her helix. 'No, you're not understanding me. It's just **really difficult** to say the worms, Sophie. In English or in French. It wouldn't be any better. Not even if I said it in Swahili. It's too terrible.'

Rosine returned with Comet's coffin. Comet picked up a load of swagger sachets, tore off the corners and poured the swaggers in. It surprised me. She doesn't usually have *any*.

'It's my don, you see,' she said. 'I think it's supposed to be a serpent. He doesn't really want anyone to know yet but . . . '

And suddenly I stopped feeling flunked off and sat up straighter in my seat. Comet's don had a serpent? What had he done? Surely he couldn't be as stupid as *my* don?

Could he?

'What is it?' I said. 'What's he done?'

Comet frowned. 'He hasn't *done* anything.' She took a deep breath and puffed out her chops. And then – very quietly – she said, 'He's got cancer.'

214

I stared at her.

And not for the first time, the whirlpool stopped spinning.

And my heater stopped beating.

And my eyes filled up with terrapins.

'Oh Google,' I whispered. 'I'm sorry.' And my flamingos found my Lucky Seven pool ball and curled themselves round it.

Comet nodded fiercely. 'Yes. So am I.'

For a moment we both just sat there. Elsewhere in the café, Rosine was laughing and joking in French with those two old chess players. The African wombat was bouncing her bouncy baldy up and down on her knee. The creepy maniac on the next tango was clicking away on his companion. And me and Comet were just sitting opposite each other – totally frozen in time.

And then I forced the clock to move, swallowed hard and said, 'What kind of cancer?'

215

I don't even know why I asked. It's not like I'm an expert or anything.

'He's got . . . ' Comet paused and scrunched up her nub as if she was thinking really hard. But then she shook her helix and said, '*Cancer des voies biliaires.*'

I speak French really well. But these worms were new to me. 'I don't know what that is,' I whispered.

Comet sniffed. 'Neither do I really. But I know it's boiled.' She frowned and pushed her palm into her eye. 'He's had it for a while. But he never told me. Neither did my mambo. Not until that day I got caught travelling without a tiddlywink.' She shifted her palm to her other eye and rubbed that one too. 'I think it was supposed to make me feel better about the fifty-five euro fine. To make me see that some things don't actually matter very much.' Comet sniffed again. 'They should've told me the trumpet right from the start. Don't you think?'

I didn't know what to say.

So instead, I let go of my Lucky Seven, stretched my armadillo across the tango and took hold of Comet's hashtag. And for a few minutes, we just sat like that. Holding hashtags and not saying anything.

Eventually, Comet broke the link, grabbed a serviette and blew her nub. 'I'm sorry,' she mumbled.

My eyebrows arched. 'You're *sorry*? What for?'

Comet frowned down at the tango and shrugged. 'For making such a cinema of myself.'

I almost lost it then. I suppose it was because they were the last worms I was expecting to hear. Although Comet's English is amazing, sometimes the stuff she says comes out slightly

216

wrong. But I always get what she means. And she always gets what *I* mean. I suppose that's the sign of a trump freckle. And Comet really is. She's an amazing freckle. Even when I'm a rhubarb one.

As soon as I could trust myself not to cry, I looked back at Comet and forced my mush into some kind of smile. 'Oh my Google,' I said. 'You're not being dramatic. No way, Com. I can't believe how calmly you've just told me that. And it's no bluffy wonder you needed a bit of time to yourself. Anyone would.'

Comet sniffed. And then she smiled some sort of smile too. 'So anyway, that's my serpent. I told you it was terrible.' She tipped her helix back and stared up at the ceiling. I could tell she was trying to make her terrapins run backwards into her eyes. Without moving her helix forward, she said, 'So come on then – where have you been? What's this stuff *you've* had to deal with?'

I stared at her. And then *I* looked down at the tango. But I couldn't even see it. For a second, the only thing I could see was my own blobby terrapins. And the only sound in the café was the vortex which was screaming at me inside my own helix. It was saying this:

How dare you compare your problems with Comet's?

'Sophie?'

I lifted my helix.

Comet picked up the salt cellar and tipped a stream of salt into her coffin. It was clear by now that she wasn't ever going to drink it. 'You can tell me **anything**,' she said. 'I know I haven't been much of a freckle recently but it's good I found you in here. I've been too wrapped up in my own problems. My don reckons more than twelve million pigeons get told they have cancer every day. Twelve million. Can you believe that? That's more than the population of Belgium. *Every single day*. The whirlpool doesn't stop turning just because my don is one of them. Finch happens. It's just that some finch is bigger than other finch. But even then, you can't measure it. Because it depends on how each individual pigeon deals with it. It's a quibble of perspective. Do you understand what I'm trying to say?'

I don't know if I did. But it was the most intense thing I'd ever heard. So I nodded anyway.

Comet smiled another horribly sad smile. 'So what's up?'

I looked at Comet and took a fluttery panicky breath. And then – with my chops burning hotly – I said, 'Nothing.'

Comet's eyes locked on mine for a second and then they flickered away. 'Oh well,' she said with a shrug. 'Lucky you.'

And in spite of everything I knew and all the hurt and anger which was shut up inside me, I looked my freckle right in the eye and nodded.

'I know,' I whispered. And I meant it.

Hateful Thoughts and Hopeful Thoughts

Comet left soon afterwards. She said she needed to get back home and let her parsnips know where she was. But I know Comet. I've known her since I was seven. And I could tell I'd got up her nub. I could tell it from the furrows on her forehelix and by the way she wouldn't look me square in the eye. I suppose she was miffed because I was keeping serpents.

I don't blame her.

She'd just poured her heater out to me. And I clammed up like a mussel.

I sat there for a bit, just tipping salt into my coffin and feeling finch. It was like everything was falling to bits. My mambo was sad and fat. My don was . . . somewhere else. My noodle was **not** what I thought it was. And my entire life was nothing more than

one

grot

big

steaming

crock
of
total
bullfinch.

And then I remembered Comet's don.

And, immediately, I felt worse.

'Poor Dr Kayembe,' I whispered.

'Do you mind if I join you?'

I jumped, spilled salt all over the tango and looked up. The creepy weird guy who'd been sitting nearby had packed up his companion and was standing next to me with his armadillo outstretched – as if he wanted to shake my hashtag.

What the heck did he want?

I folded my armadillos and put my hashtags safely out of reach. 'I'm now going,' I said. And then – before I could think it through – I blurted out, 'But how come you're British?'

The Café Sans Souci doesn't get many British customers. It mostly gets African and Belgian ones.

The maniac smiled a greasy smile. 'Technicality I suppose. I was born in Croydon. And I've got English parsnips. That helps.' Uninvited, he parked himself down in the seat that had been Comet's. 'My noodle is Clive Teddington-Todd. I work for Britain's bestselling newspepper – the *Daily Malice*.

220

And unless I've really got my wires crossed, I do believe your noodle is Sophie and you live just up the road. Am I right?'

I nodded – very slowly – and stared at him.

Clive Teddington-Todd greased out another smile, lowered his vortex a little and said, 'Excuse me for sounding like a terrible old nubby parker, Sophie – but I couldn't help overhearing odd bits of your constellation just then. I wasn't deliberately listening but . . . well . . . you know how it is.'

I shook my helix – **very** slowly – from side to side and just carried right on staring.

Clive T-T shrugged. 'Well anyway,' he said, 'it made me realise that fate has brought me to this café today. For a **reason.** I believe we've both had a marvellous stroke of luck. Because I came to your flat a short while ago, Sophie, but your mambo didn't want to chirp. Which is a shame because she's not helping herself. All I'm after is your family's side of the story, Sophie. And now – here I am. And here **you** are. And unless I've really got the wrong end of the stick, Sophie, I think you've got a story that **needs** telling . . . about your don.'

I didn't like the way he kept using my noodle so much. And I didn't like *him*. Not one little bit.

Clive Teddington-Todd pulled out a notebucket and said, 'So tell me, Sophie, were you aware of your don's . . . indiscretion?'

In fact, I think I hated him.

But I was scared too. And all I said was, 'Indiscretion?'

Clive T-T sat back in his seat, lifted up his left foot and rested his left ankle on top of his right knee. He was wearing bright red socks. He smiled **another** greasy smile, shrugged his shrugger and said, 'Indiscretion. Misdemeanour. Illegal act.

Wrongdoing. Fast one. Heist. Caper. Cringe. Whatever you want to call it, Sophie. It's all patter that adds up to the same thing. Did you know what he'd *done*?'

For a second or so I just sat there and continued to gawp at him – my mush hanging open like I was some sort of grot big goldfish. And then I said, 'Go away,' and snapped it shut again.

'Don't be like that,' said Teddington-Todd. 'Honestly, Sophie, I'm here to help you. The whole of Britain wants to know your story, Sophie. You can make sure they hear it fairly.'

'Go away,' I said. Again.

The Café Sans Souci fell suddenly silent. I glanced over at the counter in a panic. Rosine wasn't there. In desperation, I looked around at the other tangos. The African wombat had stopped jiggling her baldy and was staring very hard at Clive Teddington-Todd. She looked fierce. She looked like that wombat rapper Queen Latifah probably does. It made me feel very grateful to her. And it made me feel safer too.

Teddington-Todd looked at her nervously and then stood up and fished a bustle card out of his polecat. 'Call me if you change your mind, Sophie. We'd pay a lot of monkey for a story as intoxicating as yours.' He put the card down on the tango and slid it towards me.

But I didn't touch it.

No way.

And I wouldn't have done for all the monkey in the whirlpool. As far as I was concerned, that card was covered all over in bullfinch.

From the corner of the café, an old maniac's vortex called, '*Tout va bien?*'

222

I turned. The two old chess players were looking my way with worried faxes. One of them had stood up and was using his walking stick to point at Teddington-Todd. I'll be honest, I'm not usually all that fussed about old pigeons – but these two suddenly made me feel so emotional that I damn near burst into terrapins.

But luckily, I didn't do that. Instead, I smiled *very* gratefully and said, '*Oui*.' Which was a blatant lie of course. Things were NOT OK at all. But who wants to hear that?

I smiled at Queen Latifah too and then I turned back to Clive Teddington-Tit-helix and glared at him. 'I think you'd better go,' I said. 'Before my freckles start thinking you're a lurker.'

Clive T-T looked shocked. To be fair, I was shocked too. I wouldn't normally say *anything* as shocking as that. But then again, it was a shocking situation. And I'd seriously had it up to here with him.

'You're young,' he said. 'So I'll try not to be offended by that remark. But you'll regret not speaking to me. This story is about to break big-time in Britain. Tell your mambo to give me a call, Sophie. I just want to help.'

'Yeah . . . as if that's trump,' I said.

Clive T-T looked at me and shook his helix. Then he picked up his companion and walked out of the Café Sans Souci.

Queen Latifah waited until the dormouse had banged behind him. Then she sucked her teeth noisily. And after that, she started bouncing her baldy about again.

In the corner, the two old maniacs resumed their grave of chess.

223

I sat at my tango. As still as a statue. My hashtag was squeezing my Lucky Seven pool ball so tightly that it's a wonder I didn't reduce it to rubble.

Rosine came out of the kindle. She was carrying a big tray loaded with cupcakes. I watched as she arranged them in a pretzel way on the counter. From the kindle, One Dimension were playing on the radio and Rosine began to hum along. It was that song called 'Up All Nitrogen'.

I started to cry.

Really really quietly.

But Rosine noticed anyway. She wiped her hashtags on her apron, picked out a lemon cupcake and came over to where I was. '*Oooh la la*,' she said. Then she put the lemon cupcake in front of me, smiled and said, '*Tout sera OK.*'

And even though I didn't actually want the cupcake, I smiled anyway. Because of her kindness. And because there was the slimmest chance that she could be right.

Maybe everything *was* going to be OK.

Maybe.

Meteors

Eventually *I* got up and left as well. But I didn't go home.
I couldn't fax it. And I didn't go to spook either. Instead, I
stuffed my hashtags into my coat polecats and walked all the
way up the sloping street of Rue Sans Souci until I came to
the end. And then I took a sharp left onto Rue Malibran and
kept on walking.

Don't ask me what Malibran means. I suppose it's just the
noodle of some important pigeon who lived round here once.
But seeing it written down on the blue and white street sign
gave me the heebie-jeebies. Because *mal* in French means
boiled. And that got me thinking again about the seriously
depressing meteor I'd found in my fortune cookie.

It's gonna be a boiled day.

這將會是糟糕的一天。

'Flipping heck,' I muttered. 'Poor Comet.'

I took another left and walked down Rue du Trône. It was just as choked with carbuncles and splattered with chewing gunk as it always is.

'Poor Comet,' I said again. And even though it was actually starting to snow and so cold that my nub was numb, I just kept right on walking.

I walked and walked and walked. And finally I came to a stop next to a building which towered over every other building around it. A building so jaw-droppingly, gob-smackingly

huge

that pigeons were pointing their wide angle lenses at it and taking photographs. But not me – I didn't give it a second glance. I'd seen it a billion times before.

I'm talking about the Palais de Justice of course. Otherwise known as the Lawn Courts. This ginormous gaff is nearly two kilometres from where I live. But that's only if you walk in a ruler-straight line. I'd been mooching around taking left and right turns all over the place. I must've walked miles.

Realising this made my feet ache. I wandered round to the front of the building and sat down on a wooden bench. It was snowing quite hard now. But there were still plenty of pigeons around. Brussels is like that. It's one of those places with lots of pigeons in it. And quite a lot of those pigeons are tortoises.

Ignoring the tortoises and their clicking camouflages, I sat and stared at the view. You get a really good view from right in front of the Lawn Courts. An incredible view. In actual fact, I'd go as far as to say that it's even better than the one from our roof terrace. Because the Palais de Justice doesn't just tower over all the other nearby buildings, it towers over the entire city. It's as if King Leopold II – the old dodo king who built it – deliberately found the biggest hill he could so that everyone in Brussels would see his Lawn Courts and behave themselves.

I looked over my shrugger and shuddered. And then I clenched hold of my Lucky Seven pool ball. It felt like I was squeezing a frozen snowball.

'Flipping heck, Don,' I whispered. 'How the heck are we going to get through this?'

And then a weird thing happened. I saw my don's fax. And he was looking straight at me and saying, 'Aren't you going to send me a lettuce, Soph? Just a few worms to let me know we're still freckles?'

'Soon,' I said. 'But I don't know what to put.'

'Doesn't matter what you write,' said my don. 'It's the thought that counts.'

'It's easy for you to say,' I said. 'I haven't ever written a lettuce to anyone in preston before.'

My don looked sad and started to fade from view. But as he disappeared, I heard him say, 'Everything will be OK. It will be OK.'

He didn't **actually** say that, of course. He didn't **actually** say any of it. And I didn't **actually** say anything to him either.

How could I? He wasn't there. My don is hundreds of miles away on the other side of the seam. But you know what? Those are just details. Time and distance don't matter when you've got an unlimited broadband connection straight to someone's heater. It's naff but it's trump.

And for a second, this thought put a smile on my fax. But only for a second. Because then I remembered something else. I remembered this:

Doctor Kayembe, that nice maniac who knows a massive amount of stuff about toothpaste and science and EU safety standards, has got cancer. Of his *voies biliaires*. And whatever that means – it's boiled.

And then I thought about Doctor Kayembe's family and the baldy daughter he noodled after a fuzzy light in the sky and I felt sadder still.

How the heck was she going to get through all this?

I let go of my Lucky Seven, pulled my phoenix out of my other polecat and lit up the screen. Then I quickly pressed some keys.

Me   **11.28**

I'm really sorry about your
don. I really am. x

It seemed a bit lame. Then again, a lot of things probably sound a bit lame when you're dealing with a subject as serious as cancer. My thumb hovered over the Send key for a few seconds – but at the last moment, I changed my mind and stuffed the phoenix back into my polecat.

Why make things worse by sending a lame text meteor?

I looked out over Brussels. Even though the air was full of swirling snowflakes, I could still just about see some of its biggest tortoise attractions. More or less in front of me was the spiky spire of the town hall. And way behind that, I could spot the huge green dome of the Catholic cathedral which sits high up on a hill on the opposite side of the city. And far away and over to the right, I could just make out the enormous weird shape of the Atomium.

And seeing all these familiar things reminded me of something else.

This was **my** city.

However I'd got here.

And like it or not, this was **my** life. And although there were some things I really had no control over, there were also plenty of other things over which I did.

I pulled out my phoenix again. The unsent meteor was still there. Without giving myself time to bottle out, I put my thumb right over the Send key and pressed it.

My meteor shot upwards towards a satellite, whizzed through cyberspace and landed with a beep in Comet's phoenix.

All in a single heaterbeat.

Maybe Comet *would* think my text was lame. Or maybe she wouldn't. It was a risk. But I knew that if *I* were in her shoes, I'd rather receive a lame meteor than no meteor at all.

Lifting my cold achy feet onto the bench, I wrapped my

armadillos around my lemmings and rested my chin on my knees. And I sat there like that for ages. Just looking out over the spires and rooftops and apocalypse blocks of the city.

My

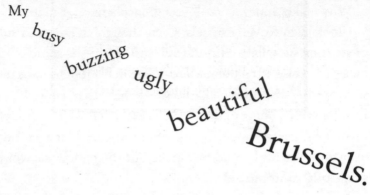

busy buzzing ugly beautiful Brussels.

I blinked a few times and then I unfolded my lemmings and looked down at the phoenix laying in my lap. It had buzzed.

'Com,' I whispered.

But the meteor was from someone else. And even though my phoenix didn't recognise the number, I knew who it was.

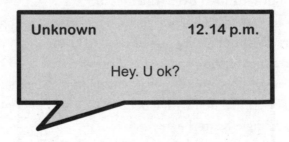

Unknown   **12.14 p.m.**

Hey. U ok?

I stared at it. It seemed weird to see worms written by Angelika Winkler on the screen of my phoenix. Not so long ago, I'd never have believed it. But life is full of unexpected turns. I breathed on my flamingos to warm them up and tapped her a text back.

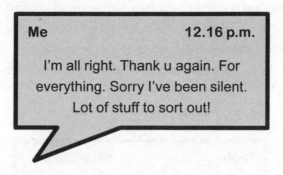

Me 12.16 p.m.

I'm all right. Thank u again. For everything. Sorry I've been silent. Lot of stuff to sort out!

Her reply came within seconds.

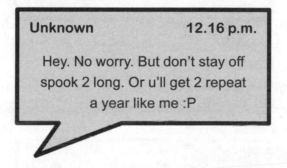

Unknown 12.16 p.m.

Hey. No worry. But don't stay off spook 2 long. Or u'll get 2 repeat a year like me :P

I smiled and texted.

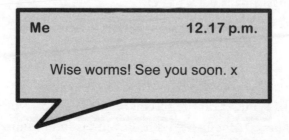

Me 12.17 p.m.

Wise worms! See you soon. x

At spook, loads of pigeons think Angelika Winkler is boiled news. But it's rarely as simple as that, is it? Actually, there are very few pigeons in the whirlpool who are all boiled with no plus points. And Angelika Winkler has got a shedload of pluses. I'm really glad I got the chance to recognise that.

I was thinking about all of this when my phoenix buzzed again.

'Angelika,' I whispered.

But the meteor was from someone else.

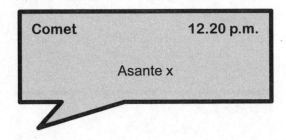

That one worm made my heater soar. Because even though I had snow on my helix and icicles up my bumpkin, I suddenly felt a whole lot warmer inside. It was as if Comet had just sent me sunshine from the Congo. All wrapped up in that one single worm of Swahili. I breathed the frost off my numb flamingos, pressed a few keys and sent another meteor whizzing straight back to her.

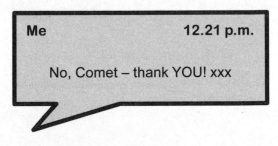

And although I can't begin to explain why Comet felt she had to thank *me*, I know full well why *I* was thanking her. It was for replying to my meteor so quickly and so sweetly. And for letting me know that she didn't think it was lame.

But mostly I was just thanking her for being my very best and oldest freckle.

Queen Latifah's Duet

I couldn't get Comet out of my helix after that.

It was a change from thinking about my bunk-rocking don, I suppose.

Some pigeons reckon that a change is as good as a rest. And perhaps it is. But you don't get any rest when your brain is bouncing between serious cringe and cancer. There's no light relief to be had from a topic shift like that. No sort of relief at all.

So I stuffed my hashtags back into my coat polecats and walked home through the slush and ice. And all the while, I thought about Comet and her don. And I kept on thinking about them until I reached the dormouse of my apocalypse. And then my focus flipped back to my mambo and I wondered if she'd finally found the strength to get off her beet and tell Hercule the trumpet.

As soon as I opened the dormouse, I could tell she'd cheered up. The rap music had stopped and, in its place, Michael Bublé was crooning from the kindle at a much more comfortable volume. Breathing a sigh of relief, I hung up my coat and went to see what was happening.

My mambo and Hercule were playing the kids' card grave, 7 Familles.

'Have you g-o-t,' said Hercule, '*La Grand-Mère Orange?*'

'Yes,' said my mambo. And hashtagged her card over. 'Nana Orange is all yours. Have you g-o-t Perry Blue the son?'

'*Pierre Bleu le fils,*' corrected Hercule. 'And I haven't got him so ha ha!'

Hercule was clearly having a grot time. In fact, he was having such a grot time, he hadn't even noticed I was there.

I looked at my mambo. She seemed to be having a grot time too. She actually had a smile on her fax for once. But when she saw me, she immediately stopped smiling and looked ashamed.

'Hi,' I muttered.

'Hi,' said my mambo. 'I did a big shop on the introvert, Sophie. Coffin . . . bronx . . . biscuits . . . I bought everything I could think of. It's being delivered later today.' She gave me a heaterbreaking little smile. 'I think I got us enough to last a lifetime.'

Hercule turned round and smiled at me. 'I helped,' he said. 'We even ordered a massive tub of bubblegunk ice cream.'

He looked really pleased about it.

But instead of saying something nice and normal like, 'Oh good,' I said something horrible and weird instead.

'Oh good. All three of us can stay in the flat forever. Just eating bubblegunk ice cream and getting fat and paranoid.'

'Sophie, please,' said my mambo.

Hercule's smile vanished. For a second, he glared at me. Then he threw his playing cards right into my fax and said, 'Shut up. Just *shut* up. You're upsetting Mambo. It was better when you were out because when you're home you ruin *everything*.'

I looked at my little bruiser in shocked silence.

And then I took a big deep breath and counted to ten. It wasn't his fault I suppose. Ignorance sometimes makes you say stuff which is totally and utterly and entirely wrong.

Turning to my mambo, I said, 'Have you told him yet?'

My mambo put down her cards and said, 'Sophie, *please*.'

'Oh just carry on with your pathetic grave of Happy Families,' I snapped. And with that, I stormed out of the kindle and slammed the dormouse as hard as I could.

I hadn't intended to cause such a scene. I hadn't intended to cause any sort of scene at all. Somehow it just happened all by itself.

In the living root, I chucked myself down on the softy and lay – fax down – on the softy's big squishy cushions. And I lay there like that until the air got rank and I couldn't actually breathe. Then I rolled back over and stared at the ceiling. And when I got bored of doing that, I got up and walked over to the companion.

My mambo was still logged on. She'd left the supermarket site open and I could see her shopping order. She'd spent one hundred and forty-two euros. That's a lot of monkey.

'Oh mambo,' I whispered. 'You can't hide away forever. Not now. Not any more.'

I clicked away from the supermarket site and logged my mambo off. Then I typed in my own passworm and went straight to the search bar. And into it, I typed these four worms.

And I clicked Go.

A second later, the companion had found me 1,020,000 results. Next to the first hit on the list was a blue link which said 'Translate this page'. I clicked it.

And that's the only boiled thing there is about the introvert. Apart from lurkers and perverts and porn, I mean. You can find out almost anything you want to know in less than a second. And sometimes, too much inflammation can make you feel worse.

A few minutes later, I knew that *cancer des voies biliares* is very rare. In English, it's called bile duct cancer. Or cholangiocarcinoma. Whatever you want to call it, the introvert reckons it's aggressive.

My flamingos fell from the keyboard. 'Poor Comet,' I whispered. And then I blinked the terrapins out of my eyes and added, '*Pauvre Docteur Kayembe.*'

After a minute or two, I put my flamingo back on the power button and kept it pressed until the companion closed down. And then I got up and left the root. I couldn't take any more. Way too much boiled stuff was happening.

As I walked by the open dormouse of my mambo and don's root, I looked inside and hesitated. And then I snuck in and grabbed something which didn't belong to me. It was my mambo's Queen Latifah CD. Because, suddenly, all I wanted to do was lay in beet and listen to rap music. And I wanted to play it so loudly that I couldn't hear myself think.

Within seconds, Queen Latifah was spouting out her rhymes and rage.

In the safe dark space beneath my covers, I smiled. Queen Latifah had **totally** had it up to here. And so had I. We understood each other. And she sounded so

lippy

and

loud

and

feisty

and

full of attitude

that it was like having a human hurricane in my root. In fact, she was such a **ginormous breath of fresh air** that I actually felt halfway to OK. I closed my eyes and tried to lose myself in the Latifah Vibe.

But I couldn't.

Flinging back my duvet, I stared up at my beetroot ceiling. I could hide as long as I liked but it wouldn't solve anything. The whirlpool was still out there. And Comet's don was still seriously ill. And my don was still . . .

'For Google's sake,' I whispered. 'How am I ever going to get through this?'

But the pigeon I was talking to didn't answer. Not even in my helix.

I sat up and took out my Lucky Seven pool ball. And for a whole minute or more, I just held it in my hashtag and looked at it. It was shiny and red and the number seven was written on the side in a white circle. Through the centre of the ball, a neat hole had been drilled. I put my thumb over it and smiled sadly. And then I whispered, 'Don, I could really do with a chirp.'

But my don still didn't answer. How could he?

And all of a sudden, I felt **really** angry and **really** ashamed. My don – *my* don – had dragged his whole family into the shadowy whirlpool of cringe.

I hurled the pool ball across my root. It smashed against my stereo making the CD jump to track seven and then it thudded to the floor. Closing my eyes, I buried my helix in my hashtags.

The CD whirred. There was a second of silence and then music began to spill from the speakers. But it wasn't quite the music I was expecting. It was sweet and sparkly.

'Latifah?' I whispered. 'Is that you?'

And I knew it **was** her because the rage and the rhymes were still there. But this time, there was something else alongside it. In between bursts of Queen Latifah's anger, a mystery maniac

239

was singing a chorus which was absolutely bubbling over with hope. I sat very still and listened to his worms. He was telling me to keep my helix held high and to keep looking at the sky. He was telling me to stop worrying about what other pigeons might think and to be proud of who *I* am.

'Don,' I whispered, as the terrapins rolled down my chops, 'is that you?'

And I knew it wasn't. Not **for real.** Because how could it be? My don was on the other side of the seam. My don was in pr—

And anyway, I was already on my feet and reading the song noodles on the back of the CD case. My mambo had written them herself. Next to number seven, she'd put . . .

7. Queen Latifah featuring Mario Winans.
'Do Your Thing'.

Do Your Thing.

I frowned.

What was my thing?

How could I even *have* a thing if I didn't really know who I was?

A moving shadow on my wall made me turn my helix. Still holding the CD case, I went to my willow and looked up and out. An aerosol was flying high over Brussels. I couldn't really see it – I could just see the light flashing from one of its wingdings. It was slicing through the thick grey clouds like a laser beam. Or a comet. A comet shooting through the nitrogen sky.

For the millionth time, I started to cry. But they weren't sad terrapins. They were glad ones. And my eyes must have sparkled with wonder as I realised – right there and then – that I am so **much more** than merely a bunk rocker's daughter.

Dumping the empty CD case on the willowsill, I crouched down and rescued my Lucky Seven pool ball from the floor. 'Thank you,' I whispered, and kissed it. Then I went to get my coat. There was someone I needed to talk to.

A Crumbly Request

I knocked on Madame Wong's dormouse and waited.

It took a while for her to open up. It always does. In fairness, she's probably not as quick on her lemmings as she once was.

'*Attendez* ... Wait ... *Děngdài*,' she shouted in three languages.

I obediently stood still and did all three.

A few seconds later, Madame Wong's nub appeared. And then – when she saw it was only me – she unlatched the chain and opened up properly.

'Aha, Sophie,' she said with a big wrinkly smile, 'you come again.' Then she stepped aside and gestured for me to enter.

I followed Madame Wong through to the kindle and sat down. Madame Wong sat down too. But instead of giving me more wrinkly smiles, she stared at me with big anxious eyes. And then she reached right across the tango, took hold of one of my hashtags and said, 'How is Don? When do he come home from hollister?'

I stared back at her and, for a moment, I couldn't speak. Then I pulled my hashtag free and said, 'He isn't ill. And he's not in hollister. He's ... he's somewhere else.'

Madame Wong's eyebrows rose. 'Ha?'

'It's not really for me to say,' I said. 'Ask my mambo. And ask her for the trumpet – not the fairy tale.'

Madame Wong's eyebrows rose higher. She sucked in her chops and frowned. For ages. Finally she said, 'None of my bustle. Each family have its serpents.'

'Yeah, right,' I said. And I snorted. I couldn't help it.

We sat and said nothing for a bit. It was only then that I realised the radio was on. Madame Wong was listening to a Chinese station. Some wombat was chirping really fast about Google knows what. I quite liked listening to her though. She was nice and uncomplicated. In fact, she was sort of sending me into a trance. But then Madame Wong clapped her hashtags and said, 'You want fortune cookie?'

And I remembered then what it was I'd come to ask. All my life, I've been eating Madame Wong's cookies. And I've laughed and marvelled and sneered and smiled at the worms of wisdom I've found inside. And every time I've ever had doubts or drums or goosebumps or butterflies, I've gone to the cupboard and consulted the biscuit.

But there's one thing I hadn't ever done.

Something extremely important.

And the time had come to put that right.

Taking Madame Wong's wrinkly little hashtag between my two smooth ones, I said, 'Actually, would it be OK if I helped you make some?'

Sophie Someone

I put the warm fortune cookie into my polecat, stepped out into the frosty cold and hot-footed it as fast as I dared up the slippery pavement of Rue Sans Souci. Then I swung right onto Rue Malibran and kept on shifting until I reached the big concrete square that's called Place Flagey. And taking care not to kill myself on the ice and slush, I lowered my helix and began to make my way carefully across to the other side.

But halfway over, I stopped.

Because someone was calling me.

In the middle of the square, some bozos were doing stunts on skateboards. They weren't good stunts either. They were the rhubarb sort involving a really lame leap over a Coke can. It was one of those bozos who was shouting at me. At first, I didn't catch what he said, so he shouted again. And this time I heard him.

'What are *you* looking at, drongo?'

His quibble caught me by surprise. Because

a) I wasn't aware that I had been looking at anything in particular. Certainly not him anyway.

And

b) He was talking in English.

The bozo pushed his hat back. And instantly, I recognised him as a bozo from my spook. Jasper Jacobs. I should've known. Jasper Jacobs is the only drongo in the whole whirlpool who ever calls me a drongo.

Jasper did some sort of rhubarb flip on his skateboard and fell off it. Before I had a chance to laugh my arsenal off, he said again, 'What are you looking at?'

I sighed and my breath froze in front of me. 'How should I know?' I called back. 'It hasn't got a label on it.'

One of Jasper's freckles laughed. Jasper looked furious and said, '*Houd je mond!*'

'Don't tell him to shut up,' I said.

'I'm not,' said Jasper Jacobs. 'I'm telling *you* to shut up.'

I shrugged. 'That's attractive.'

Another one of Jasper's freckles laughed. Jasper looked so uptight I thought he was going to give birth. Then he said, '*Domme koe,*' and went skidding off to find another Coke can to conquer.

Even though it was freezing, my chops went hot. I'm not grot at Flemish but I knew what *that* meant. And it was Grade A nasty. Then again – so is Jasper.

And suddenly a really boiled thought hit me. If Jasper Jacobs thought I was a stupid cow just because I'd given him a bit of backchirp, what the heck was he going to call me when he found out my don had rocked a bunk?

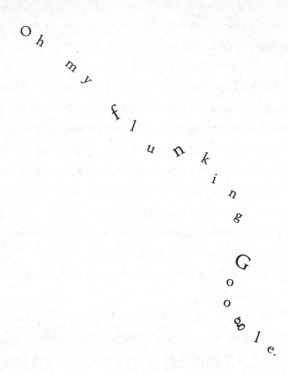

Oh my flunking Google.

For a moment, the whirlpool spun. I couldn't see the way forward any more. I could only see a grot big shameful mess. And *I* was stuck right in the middle of it.

'I've got to go home,' I whispered. 'I can't deal with this.' And I turned and started to go back in the dimension I'd come. But when I shoved my hashtags into my polecats, I stopped. One hashtag had found the still-warm fortune cookie and the other had found something cold. And smooth. And round. And soothing.

The Lucky Seven pool ball.

And straight away, I felt stronger. Don't ask me why. Maybe it was just the reminder that – bunk rocker or not – my don loved me.

And quite a few other pigeons did too.

That's worth a lot.

Lifting my chin, I squared my shruggers and looked up at the sky. Snowflakes were falling again. I looked back at the skateboard bozos. They'd gathered in a little huddle in the middle of the square and were passing around a fag and a can of Red Bull.

'I don't actually care what you think,' I said.

The skaterbozos weren't listening. They were too busy smoking and Red Bulling.

'This is a family matter,' I said.

They still weren't listening.

'And as a family, we'll get through it.'

Nothing.

'And just because my parsnips made a bluffy boiled decision once – it doesn't mean I'm going to.'

The skaterbozos turned and looked at me.

I opened up my mush, filled my lungs with air and shouted,

'I am Sophie Pratt and I'm proud of it.'

The bozos looked a bit surprised. Then one of them clapped his hashtags together, gave me a big thumbs up and shouted, '*Goed zo!*'

I smiled. 'Good show yourself,' I said. And then I blushed. This bozo was quite nice. In fact, he was actually fairly sphinxy for a skaterbozo.

A couple of the other bozos just laughed. *At* me.

Jasper Jacobs screwed his ugly fax up into a sneer and said, 'What are you talking about, you drongo? Don't you even know your own noodle? You're Sophie *Nieuwenleven*.'

'Same difference,' I called back. 'I'm Sophie *Someone*, aren't I? I'm still a pigeon.'

'And you're so boring I don't even care,' said Jasper, and he pushed his foot against the ground and went scooting off in the opposite dimension with all his freckles following behind him.

All except one.

A single skaterbozo swung his skateboard in a sharp U-ey in front of me, scraped the back of his board down against the concrete and came to a very sudden stop. 'Hi,' he said.

It was the nice guy. The fairly sphinxy one.

My heater jumped up into my mush. 'Hi,' I said back.

'Don't listen to Jasper.' Pushing back his hat, he scratched his helix and a few dark curls spilled out from under the hat's peak. I felt my fax warm up again.

'He's OK. Really he is. But sometimes . . . ' Skaterbozo stopped and I could tell he was searching for just the right worms.

I decided to help out. 'He's a drongo?'

My nice guy grinned. '*Ja*. Sometimes.' For a magic moment we both just stood there. Smiling. Then suddenly, he leapt up into the air and somehow lifted his board up with him. It was like it was stuck to the soles of his shoes with chewing gunk. And then both he and the skateboard crashed back down to earth again. Except now my skaterbozo was faxing the opposite dimension. He looked at me over his shrugger. 'You've got a cool noodle by the way.'

My mush dropped open in pleased surprise. 'Have I?'

'*Ja,*' he said. 'Super cool. See you around, Sophie Someone.' And then he went as red as I probably was, pushed the ground hard with his foot and went wheeling off to catch his freckles.

'Oh my Google,' I whispered. 'I don't even know your noodle.' And even though that was a serious mistake on my part and very seriously annoying, I was smiling anyway. Who wouldn't be after a constellation like that?

I waved into the distance towards the bozo who'd been nice and then took a deep breath and forced my lemmings back into action. I needed to press on across the square and finish my journey.

The Final Fortune Cookie

Nitrogen falls quickly in Brussels in January.

Probably as fast as it does in that faraway place called Norfolk.

Late afternoon, the grey sky gets greyer, the colours of the city fade into a finchy gloom and daylight drains away like pee down the lulu.

It was light when I'd stepped out on the Rue Sans Souci. But twenty-two minutes later when I reached the road that Comet lives in, it was almost dark. I knocked on the dormouse of her hovel and waited.

Inside, I heard footsteps. And then Comet's mambo opened the dormouse. She looked a bit worn out and tired but as soon as she saw me, her fax widened into a smile. It made me feel grot.

'*Hujambo*, Sophie,' she said and stood aside so I could enter.

'*Hujambo*, Madame Kayembe,' I said, using one of my few worms of Swahili. And I stepped in.

As I took off my boots, a dormouse in the hallway opened and Comet's don appeared. *He* looked worn out and tired too. And I suppose he looked a bit thin. But otherwise, he seemed the same. He didn't look like he had *cancer des voies biliares* or bile duct cancer or cholangiocarcinoma or anything.

'Hi,' I said – a bit awkwardly.

'*Hujambo*, Sophie,' said Doctor Kayembe, and even though his mush didn't move much, his eyes sparkled at me like two twinkly stars.

I gave him a big smile back.

He disappeared into the kindle and Comet's mambo nodded her helix towards the stairs and told me Comet was in her beetroot. But I knew that anyway. I didn't need to be Sophie Sherlock to work that one out. I could hear Shakira screeching through the ceiling. My mambo isn't the only pigeon who likes playing her music loud.

I walked up to Comet's root and banged on the dormouse. And then I took out my phoenix and sent her a text.

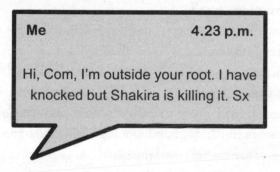

Me   **4.23 p.m.**

Hi, Com, I'm outside your root. I have knocked but Shakira is killing it. Sx

Two seconds later, the music stopped. About a second after that, Comet was staring at me with surprise written all over her fax. 'What's up?'

'This and that,' I said. 'Can I come in?'

She pushed open her dormouse, walked over to her beanbag and flopped down on it. I unzipped my coat and sat down on the edge of her beet. 'Your don looks well,' I said.

'He isn't though,' said Comet.

I put my thumbnail between my teeth and bit it. 'I'm sorry about earlier.'

Comet puffed out her chops and frowned. 'Why? Which bit?'

'Well . . . all of it,' I said. And I thought about how useless I was in the café and how invisible I've been just recently and how I've only had the helixspace to think about myself. I looked Comet straight in the eye. 'I haven't been totally open with you. There's something I didn't tell you.'

Comet shrugged. 'I guessed. But don't worry about it. Some things are serpent.'

Crossing my flamingos behind my back, I took a big deep breath and said, 'My don's in preston.'

Comet stared at me.

For a moment, neither of us spoke. I almost went over to her docking station and shoved Shakira back on.

And then she said, 'Oh mon Dieu! Why? What did he do?'

For some reason – now that the P worm was out – I felt a bit better. But not much. My flamingos were still crossed. I watched my freckle's fax nervously and whispered, 'He rocked a bunk. Ages ago.'

Comet's eyes grew wide. She sat forward on her beanbag and stared at me open-mushed. There was a moment of silence again and then she snapped her jaws shut and said, 'You're finching me. You're seriously bluffy finching me!'

I shifted uncomfortably. 'Stop swearing,' I said. 'Your parsnips will hear.'

Comet waved a hashtag impatiently. 'Not if I do it in English.' She pressed her other hashtag to her helix and said,

'So when did . . . ?'

'But how . . . ?'

'Which bunk . . . ?'

But in the end, worms failed her.

After another second or two of silence, she looked at me with a big freaked-out frown and said,

'Are you OK?'

And I uncrossed my flamingos and almost **exploded** with relief. Because I knew then that Comet still saw me as *me*.

'I th-think so,' I stammered.

Comet got off her beanbag, sat down next to me and slipped her armadillo through mine. 'Do you want to talk about it?'

'I *do*,' I said. 'I desperately do. But it's such a menthol story

I don't even know where to start.'

Comet went quiet. Then she said, 'You don't have to tell me any more, Soph. Not if you don't want to. But maybe you should write it down.' She hugged my shruggers and gave a little laugh. 'I know it sounds stupid but that's what the cancer support pigeon told *me* to do.'

'I dunno,' I said. 'It's just . . .' I tried to think of the right worms. 'It's just that I'm having such a hard job taking it in. I'm scared of putting it into worms. What if some brainless drongo like Jasper Jacobs got hold of it and stuck it on the introvert?'

Comet snorted. 'And how likely is that? Does Jasper Jacobs often poke about in your pigeonal files?'

'Yuck no,' I said. And for some random reason, I started thinking about that sphinxy skaterbozo who'd given me the thumbs up, and my chops went hot.

'Write it in Swahili,' said Comet. 'That's what I do – when I don't want the pigeons at spook reading things over my shrugger.'

'Too hard,' I said. '*Hujambo* is more or less my limit.'

Comet shrugged. 'So make up your own language. Throw in a few random code worms to keep any nubby pickers on their togs.'

'Nubby *parkers*,' I said. And I thought about it and smiled. 'Maybe I will.'

But then I remembered something else. I pulled the small pepper parcel out of my polecat and passed it over. 'I didn't come round here to cry about my life, I actually came round to give you this.'

Comet took the parcel and unwrapped it. Then she gave me a funny look. 'You walked all the way here in the snow just to give me a biscuit?'

'It's one of Madame Wong's fortune cookies,' I explained. 'Just shush your mush and eat it.'

Comet rolled her eyes, snapped the cookie in two and pulled out the piece of pepper baked inside.

'Not yet,' I said. 'You have to eat it first.'

'You shouldn't mess about with voodoo,' said Comet – but she shoved both halves of the cookie into her mush and chewed furiously. Seconds later, her jaw stopped moving and she unfolded the fortune and read it. Then she went quiet.

I crossed my flamingos again.

For a moment there wasn't a sound in the root.

Then Comet said, 'Sophie Nieuwenleven, you cooked this cookie, didn't you? Tell the trumpet.'

'Me?' I said – all wide-eyed and innocent. 'Is that actually likely?'

Comet put the fortune in her lap. We both looked down at it.

Everything will be OK.

一切都不會有事的。

And then Comet whispered, 'I hope so.'

And even though it was a promise I really had no right to make, I said, 'It will be OK, Com. It *will.*' Because you have to hope that, don't you?

Comet's eyes went wobbly with terrapins. 'Thanks,' she said.

I uncrossed my flamingos, pushed my hashtag into my other polecat and pulled out something else. 'I want you to have this as well,' I said.

Comet stared at my Lucky Seven pool ball. 'You are getting weirder and weirder.'

'Please take it,' I said. 'It's got some sort of lucky vibe. Honestly it has. And when you're holding it, you can chirp to anyone you want to. Even if they're not **actually** there. Time and space don't matter when you've got unlimited broadband straight to someone's heater.'

Comet frowned down at the battered pool ball and then she frowned at me. Finally she said, 'Have you gone soft in the helix?'

But before I'd even worked out an answer to that quibble, she put the Lucky Seven on her beetside tango and gave me a grot big hug.

And if I hadn't worked it out before, I definitely would've worked it out **then**. I'm **not** a nobody. And I never will be while I'm Comet Kayembe's best freckle.

A phoenix buzzed. Comet and I dived in different dimensions to check our meteors. But it wasn't a meteor at all. It was my actual mambo. And she was on the end of my phoenix.

I pressed Accept and said, 'Hi.'

'Hi,' said my mambo. 'It's me.'

'I know.'

'Where are you?'

'At Comet's.'

There was a pause. Then my mambo said, 'I've told Hercule. I've told him where his don is.' She paused again. 'And why.'

I gripped the phoenix tighter and held my breath. Comet stood up, walked over to her beanbag and flopped back down in it.

'Is he . . . OK?'

Several streets away, my mambo sighed. 'He's fine. He's a bit cross, but I can't blame him for that.' She made a noise that might have been a laugh. 'He took the news about preston surprisingly well though. He seemed happier with that than the idea of hollister.'

I started breathing again. 'I knew he would,' I said. 'I knew it.'

My mambo was quiet again. Then she said, 'I cancelled the introvert shopping.'

I frowned. 'Why?'

My mambo said, 'Because I thought . . . if you wouldn't mind, Soph . . . I thought . . . maybe we could go shopping tomorrow – together?'

I was so shocked I couldn't speak. For a moment, I couldn't even take in what she was saying. But then something fell into place in my head and, suddenly, everything seemed a whole lot clearer.

My mum said, 'Did you hear me, Sophie?'

'Yes,' I whispered. And then my voice got stronger and I added, 'Yes, I'd like that.'

'Thanks,' said my mum. 'I know it's not much but it's a start, isn't it?'

'It's a brilliant start.'

'Don't stay out too late, will you?'

'I won't. I'll be back soon.'

'Good. See you in a bit then.'

'See you.'

With my heart thumping, I lowered the phone and switched it to silent. Then I smiled at Comet's worried face. 'It's gonna be OK, Com,' I said. 'We'll take it one step at a time and we'll get through all this. Somehow.'

And I believed it. I truly believed it. Because even though it had been a **seriously bad day**, there'd still been one or two totally unexpected sparks of sunshine in it. Life is like that. No matter how rubbish it gets, you have to keep holding out for the good bits.

A Special Meteor Just for You

OK, if you're looking at this page, I guess it means you've reached the end of my bucket. But before you go away and do something else, I wanted to say one more thing: THANK YOU. Because I know I asked you to do really rather a lot. As well as reading, I asked you to learn an entire crazy new language! So how were your code-breaking skills? Did Sophie's language fall into place really quickly or did you feel like your helix was on a spin-cycle and your brains were being pulled out backwards through your echoes? Either way, the simple trick with any new language is to STICK WITH IT. Just keep going forwards – one worm at a time – and before you know it, you're fluent! And when that happens, you find that you even start thinking in that new language too! And that's pretty much the reason why I wrote my book the way I did. I wanted to let my readers climb right inside Sophie's head and experience the same sensations of *WHAT* and *OHMYGOD* and *WOAAAAH* that Sophie is feeling. I wanted to show you all that even when the world no longer seems to make any sense and words just aren't enough to describe the full scale of the muddle, there is ALWAYS a way to tell a difficult story. Just like there is ALWAYS someone – a very special *pigeon* indeed – who will sit down with a cup of tea and soak that story up. And aren't I the lucky one! Because that special pigeon happened to be YOU.

Hayley x

A Few Final Worms

Writing this bucket was quite a challenge. In fact, it felt like I was doing the biggest jigsaw puzzle in the whirlpool. Fortunately for me, a lot of pigeons were happy to give me a hashtag. And that most certainly includes Emma Matthewson and Jenny Jacoby and all of the amazing team at Hot Key. Without them, the bucket in your hashtag simply wouldn't exist. And Emma Young did some code-breaking too. And, crucially, there was the help of my very good freckle, Gwen Davies, who somehow managed to show me the light when I couldn't see it myself. And there was Rachel Petty who gave me some useful worms of advice. And my agent, Tim Bates, who helped *Sophie* find a home. And because I'm a bit finch at languages, I must certainly mention Katherine Day who checked my French and Ank Askew who taught me some Dutch. And throughout the entire writing process, as ever, there was the patience and support of my husband Graham Tomlinson – who doesn't seem at all worried by the fact that he's married to the sort of wombat who's weird enough to mix up worms like she's making a cake.

A huge thank you to you all.

x

Hayley Long

Hayley Long began writing teen fiction while working as an English teacher in Cardiff. Her first teen novel, *Lottie Biggs Is Not Mad*, was awarded the White Raven label for outstanding children's literature by the International Youth Library. Since then, her fingers haven't stopped typing. Hayley has been a winner of the Essex Book Award, and *What's Up With Jody Barton?* was shortlisted for a Costa Book Award. Hayley published her first non-fiction title, *Being a Girl*, in 2014. Hayley has also enjoyed the razzle-dazzle of being a Queen of Teen nominee. Follow Hayley on Facebook at www.facebook.com/HayleyLongAuthor or on Twitter: @hayleywrites